Undead Rising
Decide Your Destiny

M.E. Kinkade

To Adam, with whom I would fight any zombie horde.
And to Grandpa Jack, who never understood why I would want to write
about undead monsters, but supported me completely anyway.

Today has not been your day. First you woke up late, and had to wait behind the most indecisive person in New York—good god, how long does it take to order a tall nonfat latte with a doubleshot of caramel and no whip? Is this your first time picking out a goddamn drink? Moron.—So you were barely caffeinated by the time you made it into work, narrowly dodging a cabbie's nasty road splash (but still winding up with something indescribable and sticky on your shoes). Your boss Lisette looked annoyed, and you hid in your cubicle, hoping not to be noticed, and spent the first hour staring at your ex's photo on Facebook. Why did it have to end like that? Forget the other fishes in the sea, you two had something good.

But you aren't even able to cling to your reverie. A little before lunch (geeze, can you not even catch the smallest break?!) the first announcement came: CDC officials identified the outbreak in Chicago. It is some new virus, really dangerous. There are whispers of bioterrorism, but nobody knows for sure. It is now in New York, and probably airborne. Then, block by block, the mayor put the city into lockdown. This is serious, guys.

This is an official outbreak.

You:

⊙ Go to lunch anyway. *Turn to page 6.*

⊙ Stay indoors and raid the vending machine. *Turn to page 7.*

You've never been much for authority figures. If you followed directions every time New York faced some kind of threat, you'd have moved to Minnesota ages ago. So whatever. It's time for lunch, and you're hungry. You're going out for a slice. Or maybe you should try that new salad joint down the street?

Just as you're about to step out, Alyssa, the exuberant hippy from the next cubicle over, asks if you'd like to go to Thai Delight.

You're really craving:

⊙ Pizza. Besides, it's in the shop just outside. Who doesn't love street food? *Turn to page 8.*

⊙ Salad. As much as you hate to admit it, you're starting to lose the war against flub. You should probably watch what you eat. *Turn to page 9.*

⊙ Thai. Alyssa is a decent sort, if you can look past that she talks faster than most commuter trains. And Thai is awesome. *Turn to page 10.*

Y ou should at least respect the mayor's wishes—for now. He only needs a few hours anyway, and he'll have this crisis locked down. Once it's dinnertime, all bets are off. Besides, your office has a sandwich machine, and you never stop marveling at the way it works. Those little spirals whirring along to dispense your sandwich, the whole thing humming gently. Admit it—you're enthralled with the vending machine. It's kind of magical.

But just as you're about to smooth out your crumbled cash to feed the machine, you notice something dreadful: it's out of your favorite sandwich. There, where it should be, where it reliably has been every time you've needed it, is an empty metal gear.

You feel a little betrayed by the machine you've admired for so long.

You:

⦿ With resignation, accept your sandwich-less fate, buy a bag of chips—knowing you're going to have a hunger headache soon enough—and go back to your desk. *Turn to page 11.*

⦿ Punch the buttons for a ham on rye. It'll do. You guess. *Turn to page 70.*

⦿ Grab a slice of pizza. *Turn to page 8.*

⦿ Get a salad. At least that's healthy. *Turn to page 9.*

⦿ Rush to catch up with Alyssa. *Turn to page 10.*

Ricardo is as enthusiastic about pizza as ever. Particularly his crazy combos. He tries to talk you, as usual, into a salami-with-pineapple. You're still not interested. He wipes his runny nose on his sleeve as he hands you your piping hot pepperoni slice. Gross. But who cares? It's street food. It's not like there are standards.

Well, you should have cared. A few hours later, you're starting to sniffle, and your head is pounding. Ugh. Stupid street food.

You:

⊙ Ask around the office for some medicine. *Turn to page 11.*

⊙ Go home early. *Turn to page 12.*

⊙ Take a nap under your desk. *Turn to page 13.*

As you walk outside, you're proud of yourself. You've been saying you're gonna lose a few pounds since you made that resolution—what, two Januarys ago? It takes first steps, right?

You don't feel too bad about defying the mayor's order, because you're only going down the block to the deli; you can't be in that much danger. This is New York!

The deli is moderately busy, but it's the lunch hour, no big deal. You buy your salad—hold the extra dressing—and look for a place to sit.

You:

⊙ Sit outside. It's a little chilly out, but you'll live. *Turn to page 65.*

⊙ Elbow in at the counter, taking the last empty stool. *Turn to page 66.*

⊙ Eat while walking back to your office. *Turn to page 22.*

You meet Alyssa outside. She smiles at you and flags down the next yellow taxi. Thai Tower is only a couple of blocks away, but Alyssa is paying the fare, so who cares? You slide into the taxi after her and she gives the attractively unshaven driver the address.

"No problem," he says, in a clipped Middle Eastern accent.

Alyssa can't help but flirt with him. "Has anyone ever told you how good you look in a beard? Seriously, it's such a good look for you. Beards are SO in right now!"

You mostly look out the window. Thank goodness it's only a few blocks.

As you get out of the cab, Alyssa pays with a credit card, then slips her business card to the driver. He looks bored, not flattered. Heh. Strike one for Alyssa.

"You have a nice lunch," he says, and drives off.

She's extra-chipper during lunch. You order the pad thai, and Alyssa orders something gluten-free with tofu. To each their own, you guess.

You talk about a lot of nothing—mostly the drama from the latest hot reality television show—and are grateful when the meal is done. The food was good, at least.

Not wanting to repeat the episode with the cabbie—the first one took 15 minutes off of your lunch break, more than enough to devote to Alyssa's love life—you convince her to walk back with you. She's so busy trying to refresh her lipstick that she walks right through the cloud of smoke between two escapee office workers and gets a lungful. She coughs raggedly for a moment, and you pull her inside the office lobby so she can catch her breath. After a few long seconds of heavy breathing, she says, "Thanks. Whew. Don't know what came over me there," and the two of you head back to the elevators and to your desks.

After awhile, you notice no one else is paying attention to their work, so you quit, too. No use working extra. Bruce in IT is the only one at his desk, and you can hear him cursing at the computer.

You:

⊙ See what has halted the workday. Maybe something juicy has happened. *Turn to page 19.*

⊙ Check in on Bruce. Dude needs to chill out with the intense typing. *Turn to page 20.*

Y ou ask the office pharmacy—aka. Janet—if you can have something, anything, to relieve this pressure in your head. She rummages around in her desk, sifting through an impressive stack of vials. Her drawer rattles portentously. After five long minutes, she offers you a handful of pills.

You take:

⊙ Two aspirin. *Turn to page 14.*

⊙ A bottle of cold medicine. You start to measure out a single dose, but then decide there isn't really that much in the bottle anyway, right? So you down the whole thing. *Turn to page 15.*

⊙ A blue pill. Janet says she thinks might be an antihistamine, but then again, maybe not… Oh, what the hell. What doesn't kill you, right? *Turn to page 16.*

⊙ Nothing. You just remembered a report you heard last week about unexpired antibiotics contributing to the outbreak currently keeping you indoors. And who knows where Janet got all those pills anyway. She seems shady. *Turn to page 17.*

B y the time you make it down to the main floor, your head is pounding and your stomach churning. All you care about now is making your way home, and you're so engrossed in the rumblings in your gut that you ignore a security guard telling you not to leave. The revolving door won't turn, so you stagger against the bar of the hinged door next to it. The bar gives and you step onto the pavement outside.

You:

⊙ Begin walking home. It's not that far, and maybe the walk will help you feel better. *Turn to page 73.*

⊙ Hail a cab. No time for walking. *Turn to page 74.*

⊙ Take the subway. Might as well save yourself the cab fare. *Turn to page 75.*

Y ou really aren't feeling well, and really, you doubt you have time to do anything before you black out from the pain. Besides, your desk is big enough and the corner dark enough that you can easily scrunch under there and have a nap without anyone the wiser. You know from experience.

The office is at a low hum, but you wheel out into the hallway between cubicles and take a peek anyway. No sign of the bosses. All clear for naptime.

You roll back in and slide down to the floor out of your chair. You kick off your shoes and stretch out, hiding your face from the light as much as possible. It's not exactly luxe accommodations, but it's enough to let you fall into a soft sleep. After a little while, your low snoring dies off—along with your heartbeat.

Lisette comes by to check on your progress and pile more papers on the desk. She leans down to scold you for napping on the job—she's had her suspicions about you for awhile now, this is the last time you'll take advantage of the company!—but she doesn't get to finish her rant. As soon as she rolls you over, she can see something isn't right. When you moan "Uguuhhhhh" and bite her just above her watch, she's certain of it. Her screams bring attention, but your coworkers are a little slow on the uptake when there isn't a meeting with management to explain what to do.

Besides, the boss wasn't all that well-liked, so they don't mind too much, beyond the usual of course, that she was just eaten by one of the underlings. They do, however, get a bit more alarmed when your blood-soaked corpse starts lumbering after them.

You're a zombie now.

TURN TO SECTION Z
Page 181.

You swallow the aspirin dry and hope for the best. Your head continues pounding as you walk back to your desk, slouch in your chair, and pretend to work.

After awhile, it becomes clear, even in your distracted, head-pounding state, that no one in the office is actually working. There is a growing crowd at the glass wall. Your coworkers are staring out the window. Bruce in IT is typing furiously on his PC, angrily clicking every few moments. He is getting more and more agitated.

You:

⊙ Go to the window with your coworkers. Something really interesting must be going on out there. Bruce is always typing furiously; so what else is new? *Turn to page 19.*

⊙ Check in on Bruce. He probably knows more than the looky-loos anyway. Besides, you can't resist the opportunity to rile him. *Turn to page 20.*

The cold medicine is purple, and the lid is crusty near the top, but you've never really liked taking pills.

"Thanks, Janet, this'll do," you say, and walk away with the whole bottle, leaving Janet gasping like a goldfish out of water. You make sure you're well out of the way before she figures out how to respond.

You go to the bathroom and lean against the cool porcelain sink as you read the small print on the bottle. Looks like it's been partially used, which is to be expected, and—though it is hard to read the smudging black ink—probably expired six months ago.

Hm. If it's expired, it's probably weak, so you ignore the dosage suggestions and chug the whole bottle.

It tastes like plastic grapes. You've had better.

You sink to the tile floor and rest your pounding head against the wall, which probably hasn't been cleaned since the building went up but your head is beating like a jungle drum and you're starting to wonder if maybe taking the whole bottle was maybe not a good idea?

Against the backdrop of the pounding of your head and the roiling of your stomach you:

⊙ Go back to your desk to have a nap. It's easier to hide under there than in the bathroom, where someone is guaranteed to eventually find you. *Turn to page 13.*

⊙ Head downstairs without even stopping at your desk. You've got to go home. *Turn to page 12.*

⊙ Ought to keep pretending to work, at least. You've been saving your sick days for post-party hangover mornings. No need to waste one now. *Turn to page 134.*

"You look like you're feeling really sick," Janet says, sounding concerned. "Why don't you go ahead and take two? You'll feel better faster that way."

"Thanks, Janet, what would we do without you?" you say with a grimace as another jolt of pain shoots across your skull. You gingerly pick up two of the light blue pills and head to the workroom to get a glass of water.

You swallow the two pills at once, chased by a full cup of water. You don't drink fast enough, and they leave a chalky taste on the back of your tongue.

But Janet knows her stuff, and the pills work quickly. You start feeling better almost immediately.

Within twenty minutes, you are feeling light-headed and a little fuzzy. Your reactions slow down, and you feel like you're seeing everything through a filter. Your chest feels a little tight, like maybe you aren't getting a full breath anymore, but you don't mind it so much. You stare limply at your computer screen. Everything's okay. You're *sooooo relaxed*. Wow, what were you even worrying about anyway? Everything is *sooo* good.

And that's when you pass out on your desk, your keyboard leaving imprints on your face.

Those pills weren't antihistamines after all; they were leftover Oxycontin from Janet's husband's back surgery two years ago. And you've taken too much.

Your coworker Becky notices you drooling into the spacebar a few minutes later. Your lips have gone blue, and she shakes your shoulder but can't rouse you.

Inside your chest, your lungs forget to expand. You give a gasp as air refuses to fill your lungs. You slump down further.

Someone has called 9-1-1, but they will arrive too late. There's some kind of crisis going on outside, and your office is just too far away for you to make it, and you expire.

Janet sneaks to the bathroom to flush every pill in her drawer.

THE END

"You know, on second thought, I'll be fine, Janet. Don't worry about it," you say, and walk back to your desk.

"Well, okay, just let me know if you change your mind, honey!" Janet calls to your retreating steps.

You decide maybe some alternative medicine techniques will do the trick. You spend a few minutes Googling them, then give some a try.

You're not sure that push pins are really recommended for acupuncture, but at this point, it seems like a great idea, so you jab yourself a few times in the fleshy bit of your arm.

Great. Now your arm hurts as well as your stomach and head. Super.

All right, mediation. You sit back in your chair and try to breathe through the pain.

"Hey, everything alright?"

It's Alyssa. "Yeah, fine, I'm just trying to meditate for awhile," you say, trying to keep the annoyance from your voice.

"Oh, good for you! It's a great way to relax," she gushes. "I find it helps to sit somewhere quiet for a few minutes and chant. I like this one from my yoga class: Omm-ooouuummm-oooooh…" She is seriously droning on.

"Uh huh, thanks," you say. Anything to shut her up with that awful noise.

"Oh! I'll leave you to it," she says cheerfully. "And, you know, I'll try to keep other people from pestering you for awhile, too." She has the audacity to wink at you.

"Super," you say. Your head could not pound any harder.

You close your eyes again and lean back against the chair. Alyssa is true to her word and keeps anyone from distracting you, though over the next hour several people do walk by and look at you, sitting there motionless, with some concern.

You were meditating fine at first. But then your heart slowed, and slowed, and slowed, and then just stopped beating altogether, so smoothly you didn't even notice.

But luckily (if you want to call it that) for you, you're only mostly dead.

Alyssa comes by when she hears moaning.

"Is everything okay?" she asks, tapping your shoulder.

"Uuuggghhh," you moan. Your jaw hangs open and you drool on your shirt. You turn in the direction of Alyssa's voice, staggering to a stand. "Muuughhhh," you moan again.

Alyssa looks nervous, and backs away slightly. "Are you okay?" she asks again. The warble in her voice suggests she doesn't truly think you are.

Your head rolls to one side and you shuffle your feet, staggering after

Alyssa. She starts to scream when you grab her shirt and pull her close to bite her face. She twists away, but your fists are holding her tight.

Something heavy strikes you in the head from the back, and you half-fall to the ground. "Uuhhhghh," you say.

Several of your former coworkers are standing around you. Someone, probably Bruce, ripped the phone out of your desk and hit you with it. You moan in his direction.

Maybe it is because you haven't always been nice to Bruce, or maybe it was because he was just trying to help Alyssa, but for whatever reason, Bruce does not hold back. He kicks you.

You moan and try to grab his leg, leaning down for a bite. Someone else arrives with the fire extinguisher and bashes you in the head with it. Your neck slams backward with a crunch, and you can't pull it forward again.

It seems you made a lot of enemies at the office. A cruel word here, taking credit for someone else's work there. All those days you took off without warning so someone else had to do all your work or the project would have been behind. That raise you got that they *really* deserved more. Once people get started, they don't stop for a long while, kicking and beating you until you stop moving. Later, they'll tell themselves they were just putting down a zombie before it could get them.

But they all know why they really did it. You totally deserved it, you sonofabitch.

THE END

You squeeze in between Nick, who apparently spilled something pungent and yellow on his tie recently, and two women from accounting whose names you don't know but who look rather faint. Everyone is staring outside. It seems most of New York has decided to ignore the mayor's recommendations, and traffic is a snarl. People are crowding the street. It must be hell to get a cab. As you watch, there is a disturbance down below. It's eerie from 34 floors up, but scores of police cars show up down the street, lights flashing and horns, presumably, blaring. They aren't making any progress. In two SUVs, police in full riot gear open the doors and move stealthily toward the green-glassed office two doors down from your building. They stream inside, out of your view.

"What's going on?" you ask the general crowd.

"We don't know," the younger woman from accounting says. "But people have been leaving their buildings since the mayor's announcement, and, about 10 minutes ago, we saw smoke coming out of that building." She sounds awed.

"The one the police went in?" you ask.

"Yeah," Nick says. His tie smells like mustard. That's what it is. Gross. Nick really needs to work on his hygiene.

You:

⊙ Go back to your desk. This is pointless. *Turn to page 22.*

⊙ Go check on Bruce. *Turn to page 20.*

⊙ Go home early after all. It's not like anyone else is getting any work done, anyway. You might as well try to enjoy your day. *Turn to page 82.*

⊙ Go downstairs to see what's going on. *Turn to page 23.*

Bruce's combination of survivor-man ethos with his work-dictated computer skills makes him too tempting a target. You walk over to his cubicle.

"What the hell is going on with you?" you say, leaning in and speaking from just behind his chair.

He jumps a little. He has his earphones in, and didn't hear you coming.

You can hear the chatter of talk radio when he drapes the earphones around his neck and turns to face you.

"Things are getting bad," he says, his large muscles knotted, shoulders subconsciously scrunched up to his neck. You slap an open palm on his shoulder.

"Sure it is buddy," you say affably.

He gives you a blank stare. "I've been listening to the news reports, checking up on the situation in Chicago," he says. Does he look a little pale? "Some people are sayin' it's a biological warfare attack, from China or Pakistan or something. I mean, the Centers for Disease Control aren't sayin' that's what it is, but it might as well be."

"Biological warfare, seriously, dude? Didn't we learn anything with that anthrax scare? It's not anything," you say, sounding perhaps a bit more confident than you're feeling. "Next thing you'll be telling me the moon men are sending their laser beams to kill us all. Heh."

"If you're okay with foreign invaders taking over your precious bodily fluids, that's fine," Bruce says in a huff, "but don't come running to me when this disease or attack or whatever has rotted your brain from the inside-out. I tried to warn you!"

Um...what? "Rotted your brain? Is that what they're saying this does?" That actually sounds kinda scary and you're starting to lose your bravado.

Bruce turns back to his computer monitor and clicks through news articles, faster than you can really read them, but you see enough of the headlines to get the drift: "Highly infectious," "unknown pathogen,"—"zombie-like reactions."

Gulp.

"Okay, so what if I believe you?" you say. "Not about the warfare stuff—I mean, I don't know about that shit—but about the disease stuff?"

Bruce rotates his chair back to look at you again. "Then you had better get ready. Bad news is comin'," he says. There's an awkward pause, then he slowly turns his chair around, puts his headphones on, and resumes his furious typing.

Still trying to decide if you believe Bruce and his semi-paranoid ranting, you:

⊙ Go back to your desk. If he's right, you won't be going home anytime soon. *Turn to page 22.*

⊙ Go down to the lobby to see what's happening from that perspective. *Turn to page 23.*

⊙ Decide to do some of your own research before you let Bruce get you all riled up. *Turn to page 71.*

If you're not supposed to leave the office, you might as well get ahead on your projects. You sit back at your desk and begin working with intent for the first time today.

Sometime later, you are building a chart based on some of the numbers one of the folks in accounting sent over yesterday—you're particularly proud of the color choices on this one, they're definitely pleasingly harmonious this time—when you hear a disturbance by the elevators. There is yelling, and some kind of low—is that moaning?

You:

⊙ Roll your eyes and turn back to your chart. *Turn to page 24.*

⊙ Go see what is going on. *Turn to page 25.*

"I'm gonna go explore the building a little bit. I mean, I've been here for 3 years, and I don't think I know anyone from another floor," you say, and head to the elevator. No one seems to take any notice.

You take it down to the lobby. In the long afternoon shadows of the New York skyline, you can see people milling around outside, apparently aimlessly. At first glance, traffic looks congested, but then you realize it's not moving at all. The cars are abandoned, filling the streets. You lean on the door to try to get a better look.

"Hey, whatcha doin'? Quit that, get away from the door!" It's one of the receptionist/security guards, a young black guy you've passed every day on the way up to your office but whose name you never bothered to learn.

"Um," you say. "I'm just looking."

"Well quit it," he says. "No one is going out there. And, more importantly," he says with the confidence of a youth who has been put in charge of something for the first time, "nobody is gettin' in."

"What's the big deal?" you say.

"What's the big deal? If I let those sick folks in here and then the cops have to come to this building, it'll be my ass on the line," he says. "No thank you. We're staying in."

You:

⊙ Go over to chat with the rent-a-cop. You should at least learn his name. *Turn to page 46.*

⊙ Try to open the door. Pfft. He's not the boss of you. *Turn to page 48.*

⊙ Decide to explore a different floor and head to the elevator. *Turn to page 51.*

Now that you have resolved to actually work, you're annoyed by the interruption and keep playing with your chart. The noises stop after a few minutes, and the crowd by the window is gone. You put on your headphones. You assume everyone else has gone back to work, too. That would be the sensible thing to do.

The next time you look up, it's five o'clock and time to go. You stand up, stretch, and walk over to Alyssa's cubicle.

"So, what's going on with this alert thing?" you ask.

As Alyssa turns to you, you see her makeup is smudged and her eyes watering. Must be allergies.

"We're—we're still not supposed to leave," she says. "It's too dangerous."

"Ugh, really?" You say. "What the heck is going on out there?"

"Haven't you been paying attention at all?" Alyssa asks, bewildered.

"Um, I guess not," you say. Alyssa can be so over-the-top sometimes.

"The outbreak. It's…not just.." She sniffles. "It's infecting a lot of people. That building, with the police? Someone came in sick there this morning, and by this afternoon, an entire office was sick. The mayor sent the police to keep them in the building," Alyssa gulps. "Forcibly."

So maybe it wasn't allergies. "Are you okay?" you ask her. You don't want go have to hug her or anything, but she looks in a bad way.

She sniffles hard, snot gurgling in her nostrils. People are disgusting. "I'm okay, thanks," she says, smiling wanly. "Just a little nervous with all this outbreak stuff, you know. You're so sweet to check on me, though."

"I'm sure it'll be fine," you say, patting her on the shoulder. She stands and pulls you in for a hug. She's squishy and smells a bit like tofu. Ugh.

You:

⊙ Go back to your desk. You're not really sure where else to go, at this point. It's clear that you won't be able to leave anytime soon, anyway. *Turn to page 27.*

⊙ Gather your things. You're going home. Nothing out there can be as bad as being trapped in here with your coworkers. *Turn to page 82.*

With a sigh you push yourself away from your desk. God, what is it now?

The sounds of a tussle come from the hallway, and you lope over to investigate.

Two men are locked in combat in front of the elevator bay, grappling like clothed WWE wrestlers, but with more intensity and less theatricality.

"Hey, what the hell is going on here?" you shout as you approach.

One of the fighters looks up, arm pushing back the other man, who continues to scratch at his opponents' face. It's Samir, from Human Resources. The other guy looks like a UPS delivery man, but it's hard to tell because his khaki uniform is ripped and his shirt is halfway hanging off his chest.

"Help me!" Samir screams, panicked.

"Oh, you can take him, look how pudgy he is!" you say, lightly taunting. You lean back against the wall. "Hey, Samir!" you add with a chuckle. "What is Brown doing to you?"

"It is not funny," Samir says, his accent bouncing on each syllable. "This man is trying to kill me."

At that, the overweight package deliveryman shoves hard and pins Samir to the ground.

"Holy shit!" you say, and run forward to pull the bigger man off. "You, stop that!"

Samir is wailing quietly. "Aaaahhhh! Get him off, get him off!"

The delivery guy is rabid or something. He's trying to bite Samir, and keeps gnashing his teeth even as you pull him off.

You manage to push the guy away and Samir crawls out from under him. "Holy shit," he says, panting.

"What was that all about anyway?" you say, putting your back to the crazy delivery guy. Hopefully he's learned his lesson and will chill out for a while.

"I was getting on the elevator and when the door opened, that man was there," Samir says. "And he just attacked me. Look out!" Samir says, pointing and backing away.

You don't have time to turn around before the big man has grabbed you by the neck. He pulls back and your feet briefly lose contact with the ground. You kick your feet and manage to get to the ground again, but the crazy person bites you on the neck.

"What the hell?" you gasp and pull against the chubby man. You elbow him hard in the stomach and he lets you go with a puff of air. He says nothing, just moans for a minute. Your neck throbs, and a trickle of blood runs down your collarbone.

"AAAAAAAAAH!" Samir screams, running at the chubby man and

shoving him against the wall. He pins the man's arms so he can't grab at you, and turns back to face you. "Open the closet, we can put him in there until we know what to do!"

You nod blankly and open the door to the closet a few feet away. Grunting, Samir calls back for help. "Let's get him in there!" he says.

"Yeah, okay," you say. You haven't been bitten since that time in kindergarten, but you don't remember feeling this light-headed. Then again, it was a while ago...

Together, the two of you manage to herd the delivery guy into the closet. You slam the door and you both lean against it. The door jumps and jostles every few seconds as the man inside throws his full body weight against the door.

You feel dizzy. You must be losing a lot of blood or something, but it doesn't look that bad. You clutch a hand to the wound.

"Samir?" You say. "I'm just gonna close my eyes for a second. Do you...think maybe you could...get a doctor or something here?"

"Oh gawd," Samir says, noticing the wound on your neck. The blood has seeped down your shirt and is dropping onto the hemline of your pants. "Oh gawd, you're bleeding pretty bad!" His voice reaches a hysterical fervor.

Always one to keep calm under pressure, Samir was. The door rattles behind you again.

"Oh gawd, I'll go get help," Samir says, leaping up and running into the workroom.

When you die, you slump down away from the closet door, and the undead parcel carrier you'd been restraining stumbles out. A few minutes later, you shamble to your knees. When Samir comes back, he is greeted by two shuffling, moaning monsters.

TURN TO SECTION Z
Page 181.

You sit at your desk awkwardly. After playing Solitaire absent-mindedly for a few minutes, you get up to stretch your legs. You've been sitting too long today. You wander into the workroom, where six of your coworkers have gathered. Someone had a deck of cards, and they are playing Go Fish, though only with half-hearted interest.

You pull up a chair.

"Hey," you say. You're not sure where else to start.

There is a chorus of "hey" and "hi" from around the table. There's Kristina, who really should have worn a different shirt this morning; Becky, arguably the coolest person in your office, and your best office friend; Johnny, the hipster; Bruce, from IT; Alex, leaning heavily on the table; and Steve, who didn't say anything when you came up, and is focusing a little more intently than expected in a game of Go Fish.

It's too late to be dealt in, so you sit companionably for awhile. No one is feeling talkative, beyond the obligatory "Do you have any 4's?" and "Go fish."

Interminably, the game ends. Steve lost. He looks like he's lost more than just a stupid game of imaginary fishing. The group stares at their hands for awhile. Everyone looks dejected.

You:

⊙ Strike up a conversation. *Turn to page 28.*

⊙ Go to check up on Alyssa. You haven't seen her come by, and this group is clearly too boring for your company. *Turn to page 29.*

⊙ Have had enough. You're going to leave, no matter what it takes. *Turn to page 82.*

"So...crazy day, right?" you say.

The group stares at you as if you've got marker on your face and have all this time, you moron.

Bruce slams his hand on the table. "We are facing the biggest catastrophe of our time, we are trapped in our damn office building, and all you have to say is 'crazy day'?!"

"What?," you say. That reaction is kinda dramatic for a guy who was just playing Go Fish.

"I'm scared," Kristina says, pulling at her ill-fitting shirt.

"Look, I'm sure this will all blow over by tomorrow and we can go home. The police and the mayor seemed to have it under control," Becky says. Her voice is dangerously close to sarcastic. There's a reason you like her.

Your stomach growls. You haven't eaten anything for hours.

You:

⊙ Agree with Bruce. We need to develop a plan. *Turn to page 31.*

⊙ Agree with Kristina. What the heck is going on? *Turn to page 32.*

⊙ Agree with Becky. Things will be fine. *Turn to page 33.*

⊙ Start rummaging through the workroom cabinets. There has got to be something edible in here somewhere. *Turn to page 35.*

It's been a little while since you've seen the perky blonde, and, much as is also true of toddlers, you know there is major trouble when you haven't heard from them in awhile. Better to be proactive than to clean up the mess later.

You walk to her cubicle and lean in. "Hey Alyssa, how's it going?"

"Mmmmph," she says, not looking up from her desk. Her arms are folded and her head is down.

"Chin up, buttercup," you say, coming around and resting an arm on her shoulder. "What's got you down?"

"Mmmmughhhh," she says, as she looks up. Her eyes have a particularly vacant stare. Her makeup is smudged, making her eyes look deeper-set than usual. It's not a good look.

"Sounds like that cold moved to your throat, huh?" you ask, trying to remain cheerful. Sometimes that improves her mood, too.

She stares at you blankly.

"You look—kinda pale, actually," you say, putting the back of your hand against her forehead. "But it doesn't feel like you've got a fever or anything. In fact, your skin feels kinda clam-"

Alyssa leans back and moans full-throatedly.

"Oh, crap!" you say, backing up. "Hey guys, something is wrong with Alyssa. And I don't mean the normal stuff," you call in the general direction of the workroom.

Alyssa sways to her feet, shoulders slumped and neck floppy.

"Maybe we need to call 9-1-1 or something?" you yell.

She steps forward with a jerky motion that sends her decorative scarf sashaying. She's had bad hair days before, but nothing this bad—that's how you know she's not faking.

So maybe those zombie rumors are true.

Which means that your officemate just turned into a horror-story monster.

"GUYS," you call, more urgently. Alyssa swipes at you with a lazy clawed hand, and you easily jump out of the way.

"Alyssa, can you hear me?" you grab her hands and hold them together between you both. "Alyssa, we're going to try to help you, okay?"

By now, several of your coworkers have come out of the workroom. It's taking them long enough.

"Oh shit, what's wrong with her?" Becky asks.

"Um," you say, wrestling with Alyssa as she tries to break free from your grasp. "I think...I think maybe she's a zombie." It sounds crazier when you say it aloud. "Either that or this place has finally gotten to her and she's lost her mind."

Dodging a vicious bite, you say, "And, I'm pretty sure she's trying to eat me. Could somebody help me here?"

"What do you want us to do?" Becky says. Her tone says 'not much.'

"I don't know! Something?" you say a bit frantically. Alyssa's zombie is getting better with her lunges, and you're not sure you can continue to constrain her. "Can we tie her up or something? She's going to hurt someone."

Me, you think to yourself. She is going to hurt *me* if nobody helps me here.

Your colleagues are finally shaken from their reverie and Becky comes back with two extension cords. Bruce shoves her rolling chair into the back of Alyssa's legs, forcing her to sit down hard. You and Bruce hold her shoulders down, dodging lunging bites at each arm, while Becky ties each of Alyssa's arms to the chair with the extension cord. It takes a few minutes of wrestling, but eventually she's restrained.

You stand up and face the other five or so people gathered around the cubicle. "Some help you are," you say. They look at the carpet, shamefaced. A few wander off a short distance, as if they had something better to do than watch their coworker try to eat someone.

"So," you say, turning back to Becky and Bruce, "now what do we do?"

"She's tied up pretty well," Becky says, confident in her knot-tying abilities. "We could leave her here while we come up with a better plan."

"I'm sure you've tied her up as well as you could with extension cords, but she's thrashing pretty hard. Maybe we should lock her in an office or something," Bruce says, gesturing to the bank of closed-door offices next to the wall.

"Okay," you say, "let's…"

◉ Leave her here." *Turn to page 140.*

◉ Lock her in an office." *Turn to page 141.*

◉ Call the police. They've got to have recommendations or something." *Turn to page 143.*

"**B**ruce is right," you say. "I was just trying to lighten the mood a little."

Becky rolls her eyes at you. "Seriously?" she mutters.

"It looks like we're on our own, for tonight at least," you say. You are a little surprised by yourself. You didn't know you had this kind of leadership in you. "We've got to figure out what we're going to do."

A few of your peers nod their heads in agreement, but no one is arguing with you.

You may not be much of a survivalist, but who hasn't talked about how to best survive an apocalypse over a couple of beers with buddies? So you've already thought most of this out.

"Alright," you say, adopting a stance that you hope looks casually competent. "We need to organize our supplies and assess the situation. We'll need to find out if we've got any help coming from anywhere else— and I'm going to assume we can't count on anyone but the people in this building."

You look around the room at the scared faces of your coworkers. "Now, this will probably get hard, and who really knows what is going to happen, but if we work together, WE. CAN. SURVIVE. And that—," you pause for dramatic emphasis. That's how it happens in all the best disaster movies, so why break the pattern now? "—Is all that matters."

It's an effort to not sound smug.

"So, how about I start by...

⊙ Finding something for us to eat. We'll think better on full stomachs." *Turn to page 35.*

⊙ Going down to the lobby to see what the rest of the building is doing." *Turn to page 23.*

⊙ Sending runners to the other floors to assess our supplies and get information." *Turn to page 44.*

Though you're standing with several other coworkers, you suddenly feel cold.

"What is going on out there?" you say.

No one answers. Kristina looks at you with wide frightened eyes, and Alex shuffles his feet, intent on the carpet.

Steve, who has been moping in the corner all this time, finds his voice and says, "They're saying it's a zombie uprising! They're saying we could all get sick in a matter of weeks, and we're done for!" His voice cracks. "They're saying the infected ones try to eat you!!" Steve looks flustered and frantic from speaking so much.

Then Bruce says, calmly, "It looks like we need a plan."

It's entirely possible that Bruce has been preparing for this kind of situation his whole life. He's lean and muscular, and he's been on extreme hiking trips on several occasions. You get the impression he could throttle a deer bare-handed if he wanted to. He probably can tie knots and build a shelter out of two twigs and a handful of leaves, too.

Suddenly, you're very grateful that Bruce is your coworker. He can lead you out of this, or no one can.

Still, you're nervous as Bruce begins laying out his plan. Bruce might be excellent as a lone survivor-man, but he's never exactly shown leadership potential in the office. He's as liable to yank your head off as Bambi's.

Bruce has been talking for several minutes, but you were only half-listening. Finally he spreads his hands and says, "So, what do you think?"

You say:

⊙ "Forget this. I'm going down to the lobby to see what's really going on." *Turn to page 23.*

⊙ "I've got a better idea." *Turn to page 31.*

⊙ "Let's do it, Bruce. You make the calls." *Turn to page 148.*

"Look, this is no big deal. So we're locked in the building for a few hours, big whoop," you say, shrugging one shoulder. "If the worst thing I have to put up with is hanging out here with you guys, well—it's probably just a Tuesday. So relax, willya?" You give Steve a light punch on the shoulder and he flinches like you've removed his whole arm.

Your statement would probably have carried more weight if the fire alarm hadn't gone off just then. The air was suddenly full of the ear-piercing shriek and flashing lights.

"Well dammit," you mutter.

Your nose fills with the stale stench of urine; Steve pissed himself. You can practically see his knees knocking together.

"It's just a fire alarm," Becky says, calm. "We all know what to do. Remember when someone pulled the alarm a coupla months ago? We got out of work for a good hour while they figured out how to switch it back off again. That was a pretty good day, amiright?" She's jovial, but it's a bit forced. She's getting worried, too.

"THERE WEREN'T ZOMBIES OUTSIDE THEN," Steve yells, eyes wide with crazed panic. He has a point.

"Woah there, Steve," Bruce says, grabbing him by the shoulders and pulling him back. "Let's just go downstairs and take this one step at a time."

The siren is making it hard to talk, and it's certainly not going to help Steve calm down. Bruce has to practically restrain him to get the smaller man to move toward the stairs. You roll your eyes at Becky and follow the pack down the stairs. There are other people in the stairwell, moving down the stairs in a crowded but reasonable fashion.

The thirty-fourth floor seems a lot higher up when you have to walk down. Your legs start to cramp after a few levels.

Then the lights go out. Now you have to go down the steps led only by the light of a few cell phones people happened to be carrying. Super.

Steve seems calmer now that he has something to focus on. Still, you are sure to stay behind him and Bruce, in case he misses a step and goes down like a bowling ball.

You've just passed the 19th floor door marker when you start to smell the smoke. It smells greasy, like burnt rubber, and it's getting stronger as you move down the stairs. You look around, anxious. Other people seem to have noticed the smell, too. Some in front of you start to turn back.

"Where's that smoke coming from?" Becky mutters.

"I guess it wasn't just another false alarm after all," you say quietly over your shoulder.

The sprinklers overhead turn on, drenching everyone in cold, musty water.

Your group noticeably quickens the pace down the stairs.

Now you can see the smoke in the air, and it's getting harder to breathe. You cover your mouth and nose with a corner of your shirt.

Steve launches into full-blown panic. "No! No, I won't go down there! That's hellfire," he screams, thrashing. Bruce can't hold him back and Steve's whirling arms shove several people near him.

Bruce squeezes Steve into a bear hug and starts to carry him down. "Now.calm.down," Bruce says, teeth clenched with effort. "We're.nearly.there."

A man in soot-covered clothes runs up the stairs, past you, screaming.

You've arrived at the ground floor.

It's on fire.

The front glass doors are shattered, and the floor and furniture is aflame. The overhead sprinklers are on, but they're set too far apart, and the flames continue licking hungrily at anything not immediately under the faucets. You can just make out the outlines of people moving in the smoke.

Steve screams and breaks away from Bruce. In his panic, he runs toward the back of the building.

You:

⊙ Chase after Steve. *Turn to page 150.*

⊙ Turn and run out the front door. *Turn to page 151.*

⊙ Grab a fire extinguisher. *Turn to page 152.*

Y ou aren't the only one who is hungry. After a few minutes, everyone pools as many single dollars, nickels, dimes, and quarters they have. You open the fridge, and Becky helps you go through the contents. Bruce and Johnny inspect the vending machines. Kristina and Alex start counting the change. Steve continues staring at the table, looking dejected.

You find a bottle of ketchup, Italian salad dressing set to expire next week, half a tuna sandwich, two slices of pizza, a moldy salad, a jar of grape jelly, half a quart of milk, a coconut water, three sodas, and two yogurt containers. There are four frozen dinners, a bit of strawberry ice cream left over from the office party last month, and an ice pack. Bruce and Johnny report that there are plenty of chips and candy bars, but there are only a few sandwiches left, from what they can tell. There's enough caffeine to keep the office fueled for a week.

Alex reports that the money count is at $17.90.

You:

⊙ Portion out the foods that are most likely to spoil. *Turn to page 38.*

⊙ Declare that everyone has to fend for themselves. You quit the fast food job you had in high school so you wouldn't have to put up with shit like this. *Turn to page 39.*

"I completely forgot anyone else might still be here," Becky says.
"I think I heard a few people still here when we went to look in the vending machines," Alex says. He offers to search that half of the building.

"Johnny, why don't you and Steve check out the other side?" you suggest. Steve widens his eyes, alarmed that someone has noticed him.

"Whatever," Johnny says. "I was over that yogurt anyway."

He and Steve leave the workroom one way, Bruce goes the other. You want to start eating, but Alex gives you a nasty look when you try, so you put down the piece of pizza and wait. After a few minutes, Bruce comes back with Janet, Nick, and Alyssa. Alyssa's looking pale. Her lipstick is smudged down her cheek.

It takes longer for Johnny and Steve to come back. They found Lisette, and her assistant, Matthew.

You sort of wished they'd had to miss dinner. Now you have to be social—with your boss. Could today seriously get any worse?

"Thanks for getting us," Matthew says. "We were so busy working on the investment reports, we've barely looked up all evening!"

"You-you've been working?" Steve says. It's the first time he's spoken all evening.

"Well, of course! What a great opportunity for us to get ahead!" he says. He takes the yogurt that Johnny had been eyeing. Johnny just grunts and goes to the vending machine.

"We're possibly facing the apocalypse, and you're worried about the investment report?" Nick is flabbergasted.

"Now team, there is no reason to be critical. Matthew is just doing his job, and we'll all be grateful for it when this is over and yet we still see our positive returns on Wall Street while the competition remains floundering," Lisette says. Geeze, she's always like that. Such a stick up that ass. "I'm sure the mayor will reach a reasonable solution by tomorrow and we can all go home."

You eat your pizza in silence. Lisette claims a low-calorie frozen dinner, and Matthew has the tuna sandwich—apparently it had his name on it to begin with ("oops," you must have overlooked that). Nick joins Johnny at the vending machine and comes back with five bags of chips and two candy bars. Real healthy, dude.

After you eat, you decide to:

⊙ Go for a walk around the building. You want to see how other floors are holding up. *Turn to page 23.*

(Choices continue on next page.)

⊙ Start up a round of poker. You could use some company. *Turn to page 42.*

⊙ Check on Alyssa. She seems to have wandered off again, and she wasn't looking so good. *Turn to page 29.*

"Well, some of this food is going to spoil soon anyway, so we might as well eat it," you say.

"Like, whatever," Johnny says. Freakin' hipster.

You put the yogurts, half tuna sandwich, pizza slices, and ice cream out on the table. Alex takes back the money he contributed to the group pool and buys himself a sandwich from the vending machine; fine, jerk, not wanting to follow your plan. Before you can take the first bite of your pizza (you put the slices closest to yourself so you could claim them first), Bruce says, "Shouldn't we see if there's anyone else in the office who might want to eat?"

Everyone looks around, a bit uncomfortable that this evidently didn't occur to anyone else.

You say:

⊙ "Oh yeah, good idea." *Turn to page 36.*

⊙ Nothing, but pull the ice cream closer to you, protectively. You're not gonna share your food. It's their loss, really. *Turn to page 39.*

There's a sense of general unease at the table.

You break the silence by leaning forward and grabbing as much food as you can hold.

"These are mine," you snarl. "It's a dog-eat-dog world out there, folks, and I'm gonna be the bigger dog." Then you choke back a laugh. "No, it's a person-eat-person world now, I guess, right?" The laugh burbles out, quite mad.

Your coworkers look at each other uneasily. Kristina hesitantly reaches for the tuna sandwich sitting just outside the barrier of your arms. You growl at her and snatch it. "Git yer own," you snap.

Eyes wide, she pulls away. "Oh-oh-okay," she stutters, pulling on her ridiculous shirt again.

You start stuffing the food into your shirt. Everyone else watches in mute horror.

"Now, come on," Bruce says, conciliatory. "Leave some for the rest of us."

"Don't you get it?" you say. Now that you've let yourself go, you can't reel the crazy back in. There's no stopping you now. "We are all gonna die. Hell, we'll probably even be eaten. Doesn't that sound like fun?" You giggle like a five-year-old with a pony, then fall serious again. "Well, I'm NOT gonna let that happen to me. It's fend for yourself now, folks, and guess what? You're all a bunch of overfed sissies, and"—you break into a mad chuckle—"you're pretty much doomed!"

You stuff the yogurt container into your shirt. "Oooh, that's cold." You shiver as the plastic brushes your bare skin. "But you know what?" you say, returning to your rant, "At least I'll have a decent dinner."

You take your haul and walk out of the workroom. The low murmur of intense conversation follows you out the door.

You've unloaded your food stores into the drawers of your desk and are midway through the yogurt, scooping it out with the lid and licking the foil clean, when Bruce and Becky show up.

You narrow your eyes at them over the edge of the foil mid-lick.

"I'm afraid we can't let you have all the food," Bruce says. You don't trust the big bastard. "See, we have a lot of people we need to take care of, and you're just one person." He sounds like an after-school special. "So, I'm sorry, but we have to do this."

Bruce steps up and hauls you out of the chair. You drop your yogurt, and it splashes high up on your pant leg. "Hey, that was my yogurt!" you say.

Bruce has a really strong grip. You try to wriggle away, but his hands are giant fleshy vices. You try a different tactic. "Becky! Becky, we are friends! You aren't going to let him do this to me, are you? You can't let him do this!"

Becky gives you a flat stare, then starts opening drawers. She finds your not-very-secret stash of food and gathers it up.

Bruce drags you away. "What? NO! That was MINE, mine I tell you!" You begin to thrash with the strength drawn from frenzied fear, and you pull your right arm free of Bruce's grasp. You reach toward Becky and her pile of lunch food.

When she slaps you, hard in the face with an open palm, you are so shocked you stop thrashing. "That's enough," she says. "This is for your own good."

Bruce regains control of your forearms and hauls you away. You stop resisting and go limply with him, your arms held awkwardly over your head.

"Sorry, but we just can't have you running around scaring people like that," he says. "I'm going to put you in here, but you'll be safe, and we'll come back and check on you, okay? Maybe if you're feeling better later you can come out."

You nod. You're not speaking to him because he's a big jerkface.

Bruce lightly shoves you into an office and closes the door behind you. It's Matthew's office, and the lock has been broken for ages; Matthew never locked it, because he could never be sure he'd get out again. That makes it the perfect office jail cell.

You only have a small window into the rest of the office, but you have a wall of windows outside. You sit on the desk and stare out.

It grows dark.

There's a hesitant tap on the door, then Becky comes in with a bag of chips and a soda. "Here's dinner," she says, putting it on the floor just inside the door. "I told you we wouldn't forget about you."

You don't even turn to look at her or acknowledge her in any way. "Okay then," she says, and backs out, closing the door behind her. You don't get up until you hear the snick of the lock settling into place.

You don't eat the chips until you have arranged each one by size, smallest on the left, largest on the right. This is complicated because it's so dark, but you persevere.

Sometime in the dark, you hear talking outside. You hear moaning, like many voices lifted in a macabre chorus. Voices grow alarmed, and then screaming. You hear yelling and thumping sounds. Once, something slams into your door, causing it to rattle in the hinges.

You get up excitedly and shake the handle, trying to escape. The door is still locked tight. Outside, you see many shadows, some very slow and walking off-balance, others running or falling. You rattle the door but no one pays any attention to you.

By the time the sun rises, the only sounds left are the quiet moans. You can see now that they come out of people you don't know, people who look barely held together. Some of them are missing limbs. Most are covered in drying blood.

You rattle the door and yell, but they pay you no attention. You pull on the door, but you can't get out.

No one comes to your rescue. For a full desperate week (you count nightfalls, keeping a tally you carve into the desk), you starve. Finally, dehydrated and exhausted, you fall asleep and do not wake again.

THE END

You keep a pack of cards in your desk for just such an occasion—granted, you hadn't really planned on the whole "trapped in the office with a bunch of coworkers" thing, but there's always time for a game.

You bring out the cards for the nervous bunch at the table. "Anybody up for a game of poker?" you say, forcing enthusiastic cheer into your voice.

It takes a few minutes of cajoling, but eventually you convince most people to play.

Kristina and Steve have never played before, and you spend quite a few minutes explaining the point. Kristina cottons on quickly; Steve seems mistrustful of everyone, and his eyes dart continually over the top of his cards. He telegraphs his tell like a lighthouse beacon.

You're starting to clean up nicely—which would be a lot more impressive if you were playing for something other than paperclips and rubber bands—when Lisette's toady Matthew oozes into the room.

"Poker?" he says, sounding mildly disgusted. "This is the best use of your time?"

"We were more than enjoying ourselves until just a moment ago," you say. You tap the table for current-dealer-Kristina to hit you.

"Please," Matthew says. "You're playing for paperclips. What kind of fun is that?"

"Sorry we aren't proving sufficiently stimulating," Becky says, dry as ever. "You could always let us know what else we could bet with around here." She's rolling her eyes at Matthew with a bit of malevolence as she shows her hand—her three-of-a-kind Jacks win the pot.

"If you're going to play such a rudimentary game as poker—"

Before Matthew's even done speaking, you've started to snarl.

"—you might as well play a proper game. Lisette's got some wine in her office. Let's make this a real party," Matthew finishes. You're feeling a little less like snarling, but...only a little.

"Let me get this straight—you want to play in exchange for Lisette's wine?" you ask.

Matthew gives you a flat stare. "Subtlety has never been your strong suit, has it? Yes, let's play."

The game is a bit dry. And nothing satisfies boredom like a couple of drinks. So you agree; besides, the alcohol will help you tolerate Matthew's presence.

He wasn't kidding about there being wine. It was high-class stuff, about 10 bottles. Apparently Lisette had a habit of hoarding it for her important clients. Bruce also had been hiding three-quarters of a bottle of whiskey in his desk, which he brings out to share. Your little group makes quite a nice party out of the liquor and too-small Styrofoam cups, and the game of poker devolves fairly quickly into a game of strip poker.

You don't play as well when you're drunk, which is why you are half-naked when the elevator BINGs and empties out its load of undead, human-eating cargo.

When the first shambler wanders into the room, you laugh hysterically. "Look!" you yell, pointing grandly. "Look, at iss hair! I knew that orange floof wasth a piece!"

The balding banker in an overpriced suit moans at you and shuffles forward, sausage fingers extended in your general direction.

Your laughter triggers nausea, and you proclaim, "I feel shick," seconds before you vomit your guts onto the banker's shiny shoes.

He doesn't even slow down. He matter-of-factly bends down and bites you on your naked lower back while you hurl.

"OW!" you yelp, drunkenly trying to shove him off. "You're FIRED!" you say, and giggle at your own joke, already forgetting that you're bleeding.

Kristina tries to get out of the room, but trips on the legs of the chair in front of her and falls flat on her face as a corporate executive zombie moans into the door.

Steve just sits there and wets himself, and he didn't even drink, the party pooper.

A few hours later, you and your partially nude coworkers have joined the shambling herd. Next time, maybe you should rethink drinking on the job.

TURN TO SECTION Z

Page 181.

You're feeling pretty confident about your plan. Maybe this will actually turn out to be a good thing. You can be a hero or something. Just look at you, Hero of the Year! Savior of the City!

You send Steve and Nick upstairs with a pen and a pad of paper, with instructions to find out how many people are on each floor and what kind of supplies they might have. You figure they're probably safe going up; it's fewer floors, and you're mostly looking for a way they can actually be useful instead of dead weight.

The choice of who to send downstairs is more important. Ultimately, you decide you need two groups, dividing the building into rough thirds. You send Bruce and Alex down to the bottommost floors—they're probably the best able to manage the stairs, and, if anything goes wrong, they can fight back.

You assign Kristina and Becky the middle section. All three groups take the stairs, even though it's a long way down for Bruce and Alex, because you're worried the power may go out at any second.

You stay on the floor to sketch out a rough shape of the building, including entrances and exits, on a white board. You're gonna need a solid plan if you're going to survive something as dangerous as you suspect this is.

Becky and Kristina are back first. Despite their head-start and the relative ease of their assignment, Steve and Nick don't return for another 20 minutes. Bruce and Alex turn up a few minutes later, panting. One of Bruce's sleeves is torn from the elbow to the wrist. Alex's forehead is bloodied.

"We've got a problem," he says.

They were attacked by the venture capital group on floor two, who had armed themselves with knives and at least one gun. They had heard moaning when they had gotten near the lobby, and it looked like the front doors had been broken, but they could only risk a peek—it looked bad down there.

Otherwise, the building is fairly hospitable. The cafeteria on floor eight seems well-stocked, and the biomedical lab on floor 21 had a lot of "fizzy stuff and jars." (Kristina isn't so good at description, it turns out.) Several of the floors are empty, just offices and desks.

Well, fearless leader, now what?

⊙ Be reassuring. Tell them everything will be okay. *Turn to page 33.*

(Choices continue on next page.)

⊙ Um, maybe you're not really cut out for this leadering thing after all. *Turn to page 148.*

⊙ Time to put your game face on. Let's do this. *Turn to page 163.*

"So you've been watching what's going on out there all day?" you ask as you walk up to the semi-circular desk.

"Yeah," he says. "It's been sorta a crazy day. I mean, at first it was New York as usual. But then there was that thing with the cops down the street, and now traffic is so backed up, people are just abandoning their cars. It's trippy."

He looks about 19. You introduce yourself.

"Yeah, I seen you come in. 34th floor, right?" he says. "I'm Douglass. With two s's."

After a pause, you say, "Sorry I never introduced myself properly before." Awk-ward.

"It's no big, it comes with the turf. The only people who speak to me usually are lost tourists."

You chuckle.

"So, what's your plan, Douglass? Are we going to stay in here forever?" you ask.

"I dunno," he says. "Honestly, I expected to get some more news by now. I've been listening to the radio all day. You wouldn't believe what they're sayin' is goin' on out there."

"Oh yeah?" you ask, interested.

Douglass drops his voice and leans in conspiratorially. "They're sayin' we've got an honest-to-god zombie invasion."

You roll your eyes. "Yeah, and which 'they' is saying that this time?" Shock jocks will say anything. Maybe someone pulled some kind of *War of the Worlds* shit and freaked the whole city out. Heck, maybe it was all a hoax from a rogue Twitter account.

"It's all over the radio. The mayor, he's soundin' scared, dude, and there hasn't been a report from him in a coupla hours. And how else do you explain the people in the streets?"

Douglass had a point, there, but then again, this was New York. Who knew what was going on any given day?

"Zombies, huh? Like, eat-your-face-off monsters?" You are really having trouble believing this. Either the kid is gullible, or he's pulling your leg.

"Nah, like, it's some kind of disease like Mad Cow or some shit that eats these holes in your brain," he says. "And, like, makes you, yeah, like a zombie you'd see in a movie or whatever."

"Riiight Douglass," you say. "You've been doing a bit too much PCP, dude."

"I'm serious!" he insists.

He must be gullible, then.

You:

⊙ Mutter "He is gonna hate being so freakin' stupid in the morning when this whole thing turns out to be a sham," as you head back to the elevator bay. *Turn to page 51.*

⊙ Decide to try the front door. You'll just show him it's all fake and the whole building will be able to go home. You'll be the goddamn hero of the building. *Turn to page 48.*

⊙ Try to formulate a plan for the evening with Douglass. He's got to know about every floor in the building, and maybe even how many people are still here. *Turn to page 52.*

⊙ Go back upstairs to tell your coworkers what Douglass told you. *Turn to page 54.*

You turn and stare straight at the security guard for a moment, letting your eyes bore into his. Then you turn back and slowly, steadily, push on the door.

Your moment of glorious rebellion is temporarily hampered—the handle doesn't budge. You glance down and shake it, embarrassment feeding your anger, and the bar clicks and moves down.

"Ha ha!" you yelp, joyous.

"Hey, don't do that!" the guard says, hurrying out from behind his desk. "What the hell do you think you're doing?!"

"I," you say, opening the door, "am going out."

You walk through the door, triumphant.

"Your mistake!" the young security guard says as the glass door closes after you. His next words are distorted through the glass: "Can't say I didn't warn you."

He pulls a metal tool from a keychain on his belt and does something to the door, making the push bar pop back up. He rattles the door; this time, it doesn't budge. You watch for a moment as he walks down the row, repeating his process for the other doors to the building.

Pleased with yourself, you start walking down the sidewalk. You're nearly whistling to yourself. You nod to a woman carrying what look like heavy bags and walking briskly; you're a bit confused by the look of pure horror on her face, but you continue walking in the direction she was leaving.

As you pass an alleyway, you hear a low moaning. You were mugged once—the thugs took your watch and your new cell phone—and you remember what bruised ribs feel like. You lean in: "Hello? Are you okay?"

A low moan is your only answer. You can see someone standing hunched over further in, but you can't see what might be wrong or if he (or is it she?) is hurt. You take one step into the shadows. "Hey, do we need to get you to a hospital or something? I can call an ambulance," you offer.

The person staggers forward. You can almost make out some kind of dark stain near the abdomen—you'd be groaning if that happened to you, too.

"Okay, let me help you," you say, walking toward the hurt person. He has shaggy dark hair and he looks like maybe he's been living on the streets for awhile; at any rate, his clothes are dirty and his eyes are sunken. You take him by the elbow and guide him toward the light. He doesn't say anything, but sort of leans down closer to you.

"That's it, I'll help you. Let's just get you in the light so I can see what's wrong," you say.

A moment later, you both step into the sunlight, and you peer intently at this victim. "Okay, it looks like you have some kind of bite wound," you say. "Did a dog bite you or something? I'll call 9-1-1."

The man moans, and looks like he might faint. You move to catch him… only to realize that he wasn't fainting, he was lunging. Toward you.

"Woah, there, that was uncalled for," you say, pulling back. You're still listening to the ringing tone for emergency services. "I'm trying to help, buddy!"

The man bares his teeth and lunges for you again.

Realization dawns on you.

"Holy shit," you say. "You're one of those infected—oh my god I'm standing next to a zombie!"

You turn and run back toward your building, your phone still ringing incessantly in your hand. The zombie shuffles after you.

When you reach the front glass doors of your office, you pull on the handle, trying to get back in. The security guard stays seated behind his big desk.

"What did I tell you?" he says. "I told you not to go out."

"Ohmigodpleaseletmein!!!!" You're a bit panicked now, and you rattle the door, hoping it'll give and let you back into the safety of the interior. "I'mserious, pleaseletmein," you say, words tumbling over one another.

"Changed your mind, huh? Decided maybe you should have listened to ol' Douglass, eh?" the young man starts to get up from behind his desk and saunters in your direction.

Your noise is attracting attention—it seems the…thing… you encountered in the alley wasn't the only one. Several more people-shaped monsters shuffle out of the traffic, which is at a dead stop. You see them coming in the reflection on the glass and start to cry. "Omigod!"

Douglass also notices the other people behind you, and stops and stares in disbelief. "So what they're sayin' on the news is true," he says slowly, amazed.

"Yes please, please let me in!!!" you say, rattling the door again.

The zombies shuffle closer.

Douglass jangles his keys, trying to find the tool to unlock the door. He crouches down to look up into the lock, and tries to fit the thin metal pole into the mechanism.

It seems to be stuck.

Someone is breathing—or rather, moaning—down your neck.

You turn around and stare face-to-face with a tattooed woman. Her decorated arms now feature a large gaping wound high on her right shoulder. She reaches toward you.

"Hey man!!" you yell, "hurry!"

The zombie woman grabs your arm and tries to pull you toward her. You fight back, pushing away with all your might, but the glass door is behind you. You don't know what could be taking Douglass so long.

"HELP ME!" you scream, pounding on the door like a toddler in a temper tantrum. "OH MY GOD HELP ME!"

You're still screaming when the zombie bites you.

Douglass had his hand on the latch, ready to let you in, but, seeing your injury, he flips the lock back in place.

"I'm sorry," he says, horrified. "On the news, they said, they said don't let anyone who has been infected come near you. I can't…I can't let you in."

Your eyes go wide with fear and the blood running down your neck. "OH MY GOD PLEASE, HAVE MERCY!" you cry.

Douglass just stares at you and backs away. His eyes don't leave yours as you are dragged back into the crowd of undead monsters.

TURN TO SECTION Z
Page 181.

Y ou board and pick a number at random.

You push:

⊙ 40. Up to the roof! If you can't get out the front door, you might as well try to get some fresh air. *Turn to page 55.*

⊙ 3. It's the magic number, after all. *Turn to page 56.*

⊙ 21. Dead-center, plus one for spice. *Turn to page 57.*

⊙ Floor 34. Old habits die hard. *Turn to page 54.*

"So Douglass with two s's," you say, "what do we do about this zombie outbreak?"

"Shit, I dunno. I've been sitting here watching my desk and making sure no one goes out like the mayor said, but we didn't exactly go over zombies in our trainin' manual," he says. For someone who just told you all hell is literally breaking loose outside, he seems pretty casual about it all.

"Alright then Dougie," you walk behind the desk and lean on the edge, peering into the small flickering security monitor. "Let's start with what we do know. How many people are in the building?"

"'Bout 200 came in today. Some left first thing, before I could lock the doors, but that's a reasonable guess."

"Any floors that might be particularly helpful in, say, fending off a bunch of monsters? Any supplies or whatever?"

"There's a bunch of hammers and shit like that in the basement, probably some lumber and stuff like that. Oh, and floor 35 is under construction right now, so they maybe left some of their tools. Other than that, lessee, there's the janitorial supply co., probably not that helpful though maybe we could build, like, a bomb or somethin', and uh, oh yeah, that med supply company. Maybe they're building a anecdote or somethin'?"

"Antidote?"

"Thass what I said. A cure or shit like that, like in one of them Crichton movies."

"Yeah, maybe you're right about that." The kid really is gullible. This is what is considered security these days? Geez. "How many ways in are there?"

"In the building? Uh that's about three, not including the helicopter pad Mr. Lee's got on the roof, and the two fire exits."

"Wait, what? Helicopter pad?"

"Oh yeah, big-wig on 40th floor, Mr. Lee? He got this wicked-cool helicopter on the roof. I saw it once." Douglass is still glowing with envy.

"Okay, so basically we've got a bunch of probable construction equipment, some chemicals, and a helicopter?"

"Yeah. And a bunch of accountants and marketing folk and whatever, but I figure they're not much help right now, unless you wanna advertise an end-of-world special or sumthin'."

"Funny, kid. Real funny."

You:

(Choices continue on next page.)

⊙ Go talk to your coworkers. They were more useful than this kid. *Turn to page 54.*

⊙ Head for the roof. You need to see if this helicopter is real. *Turn to page 55.*

⊙ Have just the idea to save this building. *Turn to page 170.*

You arrive back in your workroom, breathless. You rest your hands on your knees for a few minutes, catching your breath, then open the door to the rest of the office and call out, "EVERYONE, PLEASE COME TO THE WORKROOM IMMEDIATELY. I HAVE URGENT NEWS."

There is some general muttering and moaning, but you ignore it and return to the workroom. Slowly people filter in. When you have a majority, you begin explaining what you saw.

"So you're saying we are dealing with—with zombies?" Becky asks, incredulous.

"I know, it sounds crazy, but it's true. That's why we can't leave. That's why the Centers for Disease Control were involved. It's some kind of biological agent," you say, talking so fast you stumble over your words.

"My God," someone near the back says.

"What are we going to do?" says Steve, sounding mildly panicked.

"I've got to call my husband," Kristina says, and bolts out the door.

The room fills with an awkward tension.

You say:

⊙ "I've got a plan." *Turn to page 31*.

⊙ "Does anyone have any good ideas?" *Turn to page 148*.

⊙ "Hey… has anyone seen Alyssa?" *Turn to page 29*.

U p up up, away you go. You jam to the elevator music a little; smooth jazz. Who picks the elevator music, anyway? Is there an elevator-music-DJ somewhere?

You've got time to wonder. The elevator stops on other floors twice, but no one is there either time. One floor is some kind of publishing company, with elegantly blocked letters, the other a funky software company. You can tell because they used a lot of wild colors to paint the lobby to "inspire" their people. Must be nice to work somewhere where they care about your creative self. You felt burned out at your job after 20 minutes.

The doors open on the 40th floor. Your building is tiny compared to some of the big boys in the city, but you still get a decent view of the river up here, so the top floor is considered primo property. You've never been up here before, but everyone in the building knows the top is controlled by an ad agency. It's tastefully decorated in the lobby, with plush couches and blown-up examples of their ads, going back all the way to the 1950s. You hear voices quietly in the other room, but you don't really want to chat with these assholes. You're on a mission.

You're not here to lounge.

You try an unobtrusive door; the only one nearby that doesn't have a window looking in. A small sign, no bigger than a business card, says "Roof Access." It's heavy and, evidently, locked.

You:

⊙ Look around for a key. You are going to get on this roof, damn it. If that means you have to talk to the ad men, well, so be it. *Turn to page 59.*

⊙ Give up and try to explore another floor. *Turn to page 51.*

⊙ Go back to your floor. Oh well. *Turn to page 54.*

The elevator doors open onto a world made of white tile and steel machinery, and a sea of faces topped in tall white hats turns to stare at you.

If this is the end of the world, this really might be Hell's kitchen.

"Excuse me, can I help you?" A short woman in a red coat has walked up out of the massive kitchen toward you.

"Um," you say eloquently. "What is this place?"

"This is Hibachi-1-2-3. Are you here for a lesson?"

"Oh, no, um, no," you say. You've interrupted a class. Satisfied that you're being taken care of, the rows of students turn back to their sizzling griddles. "This is a hibachi school? That's so cool."

"Mm," the short woman says. "Why are you here again?"

You step off the elevator, much to the woman's chagrin. "Oh, you know, just exploring the building since we're not supposed to leave. I've worked here for four years and I had no idea there was a hibachi school in the building."

You peer at a chef practicing throwing an egg-shaped wooden model into his hat. "Huh, so that's what they do. Hey, miss? Do you give out samples or anything?"

"You may call me Chef." She doesn't sound amused. "And no, we do not give out samples. Now please leave, you are interrupting my lessons."

You glance down and realize that Chef is holding a long, dangerous-looking cooking knife at her side.

"Ooh-kay then, nicetameetcha, buhbye!" You can't press the elevator button fast enough.

⊙ Never mind, this floor is lame. They don't even give out samples? Back to the elevator. *Turn to page 51.*

The elevator opens into an incredibly small lobby—not much bigger than the closet in your matchbox apartment. You're facing another door, something heavy and metal. The words "Ziggurat Laboratories" are emblazoned in the metal, the G's swirling into themselves. A slogan below says "Unearthing new discoveries, step by step."

You knock.

You stare at your feet, shuffling awkwardly. You feel the walls closing in on you a little. You think about maybe getting back on the elevator. Maybe the walls are shrinking, like that one room in *Indiana Jones*. Or *Star Wars*. But you're no Harrison Ford. You start to panic.

A buzzer sounds, the metal door clicks open. You try to hide your sigh of relief.

This room is not much bigger than the last, but there is a man in a blue plastic jacket on the other side of a glass window.

"Hi, I'm a neighbor, I guess you could say, from floor 34," you say. You didn't really think this whole process through and you're babbling. "Just thought I'd come say 'hi'."

"Well hello!" the man says. "I'd shake your hand, but then we'd mess up the safety protocols. And there's also this window between us." He knocks on the glass and offers an aw-shucks smile.

"Heh, yeah." He seems to think he's being funny? "We didn't have much to do on our floor, so I figured I'd just wander around for awhile. What do you do here?"

"Oh lots of things, lots of things. You can call me Jim, by the way." That big grin again.

You introduce yourself. "So what's with the glass and big metal door and all that?" you ask Jim.

"Oh, we just do some low-level bioterror stuff, you know, like your basic infectious diseases and whatnot. That's why you'll have to stay out there, neighbor!" Jim laughs again. You're starting to think maybe he's been breathing in chemicals for too long.

"Well, nice meeting you, I guess," you say, and turn to walk away.

A thought occurs to you and you pivot on your heel. "Say Jim? You have any idea what's going on with this disease outside?"

The smile falls from Jim's face. "Yeah. We sent a sample to the CDC last week when we got some odd mice in a shipment. I don't know what it is, but all the mice are dead. It's not pretty."

"Wow, that sounds pretty intense, Jim."

The smile pops back up. That thing must be attached with a bungie cord or something, it's so springy. "Oh, I'm sure it'll be just fine!" Jim says. "Dontcha worry! Even when the mice died, they got up again!"

You can't leave quickly enough. The maniac laugh follows you out the metal door.

⊙ Explore a different floor. *Turn to page 51.*

Y ou stride past the ad agency's glass door like you own the place. The
receptionist abandoned the desk; you hear voices, but can't see anyone
in the labyrinthine cubicle farm.

"Hey, anybody up here know how to get to the roof?" you call, leaning
around the receptionists' desk. You wait a half beat then begin rifling
through the drawers, thinking maybe there's a key in there somewhere.

"Can I help you?" The speaker is a sharp-dressed older man, Japanese
maybe?, and even though he isn't large, he projects power. He's used to
being listened to.

"Ugh, hi," you say. "I was just looking for a key to the roof or
something." You feel a little sheepish that you were caught.

"Mm, hm," he says. "If you'll stop invading the personal property of
my employees, perhaps I can help you."

"Right, sorry," you say, backing away from the desk. "Wasn't sure
anyone was even here, heh..heh…"

He stares at you under severe eyebrows. "I'm Charles Lee," he says,
extending a hand. "Mister Lee to you."

"Mr. Lee, happy to meet you," you say, and offer your name in return.
"Nice place you've got up here," you say. You're never good in situations
like this. "I've always wanted to see the view from up here."

"Perhaps I can help you with that," he says. "I'll get the keys from my
office. Follow me."

You follow him through the warren of cubicles. Mr. Lee's employees
are gathered around a big-screen television mounted on a wall in a common
area. They're wearing expensive suits, and are in various states of undress, a
tie loose here, a shirt untucked there. They're leaning on desks or sitting
cross-legged on the floor, staring intently at the screen. They must have a
coffee bar up here, because everyone has a cup in their hands or
somewhere nearby. Lucky bastards. Lisette would never pay for something
like that.

Mr. Lee has, of course, a corner office. He has an immense view, and
faces away from it. When you've got luxury, you don't even need to
acknowledge that you've got it. His desk is expensive, impressive, and
completely lacking in storage compartments of any kind. It's also
immaculately clean, aside from the slim expensive computer and a single
fountain pen. There doesn't seem to be, however, any paper in evidence.
You wonder what he writes on with his fancy pen.

He opens a drawer on a black filing cabinet tucked against the near
wall and pulls out a large ring of keys.

"Why," he asks you, "do you want to go to the roof?" The way he
stares at you is a little intimidating. And by a little, you mean a lot. A lot
intimidating.

"Ugh, just to see what's out there, I guess," you say. "And it's not like we can go out the front door, anyway."

"Mm," he says. He presses his lips into a tight line. "Well then. Would you like company?"

You say:

⊙ "Sure, why not?!" *Turn to page 61.*

⊙ "No thanks. I'm flyin' solo." *Turn to page 63.*

⊙ "You know, I just remembered I'm afraid of heights, so, I'm just gonna go back to the elevator…" *Turn to page 51.*

Y ou may be intimidated by Mr. Lee, but he's letting you go on the roof, so you're going to go ahead and put him in the "friend" zone. He leads you back to the locked door and opens it after rifling through his keys for a moment. He has many. There's a stairwell, painted in that ubiquitous tan color used in the stairwells of every office building ever. Someone must have offered a good discount on stairwell paint.

You climb up, Mr. Lee behind you, feeling a bit awkward because you only just met the guy. What's the script for a situation like this?

"So, what is your plan for this disease situation thing?" You're so eloquent under pressure.

Mr. Lee doesn't answer until you're at the top of the stairs, pushing open the door. He stops in the doorway and says, "Well we certainly weren't prepared for this situation." He's dour. "I suppose we're going to stay in the building…unless I decide to take my helicopter away from here."

He sweeps his arm to the right, turning away from you, indicating a beautiful red helicopter resting on a landing pad.

"Woah! Is that a real helicopter? Can I sit in it?!" You don't even bother to hide your unabashed enthusiasm. Man, helicopters are cool.

"I think not," Mr. Lee says icily.

"So that's why you have a key to the roof in your office," you say, running your hands along the sleek exterior. "Do you actually commute in this thing?"

"On occasion," Mr. Lee says. He grimaces. "I'd appreciate it if you didn't foul it up with your oily fingers. It looks like it won't get washed anytime soon, and I don't enjoy fingerprints on my windows."

"Oh, sorry," you say, and put your hands in your pockets. You peer into the cockpit, standing on tiptoe to look in. "Do you fly it, too? Or do you have, like, your own pilot?"

"I can fly it," Mr. Lee says. "But for the most part I leave that to my pilot, yes."

"Can we ride in it?" You are practically jumping to climb in.

Mr. Lee walks over and puts his hand protectively on the side of the helicopter, subtly moving his body between you and it. "I don't think that would be appropriate at this time."

You sigh and turn away from the helicopter, disappointed.

You were so excited about the helicopter that you completely forgot why you walked up here, but now you remembered that you're supposed to be checking out the scene below. From where you are standing, between the helicopter and the building's water tower, all you can see are the sides of taller buildings all around you. That and that it's a beautiful day.

You look longingly at the helicopter and:

⊙ Walk the periphery of the roof. *Turn to page 90.*

⊙ Go back inside. Nothing up here could possibly be as cool as the helicopter. *Turn to page 91.*

"I see," Mr. Lee says. "And why should I give you the keys, again?"

"Because…you're nice and I just want to get some fresh air after being stuck in this damn building all day?" Okay, even to you, it sounds pretty stupid when you say it out loud.

"I suppose I can understand cabin fever," Mr. Lee says after a long pause. "But I'm not letting you go up alone."

You begin telling yourself all the ways Mr. Lee sucks when he adds, "My pilot Ms. Mellencamp will assist you."

Your jaw drops at the words "my pilot," and you're too dumbstruck at the idea to say anything, so Mr. Lee walks away without another word. A moment later, a thin, obviously strong woman with a short red bob walks over and shakes your hand vigorously. "Hi there," she says. "I'm Genevieve Mellencamp. You can call me Jenny, regardless of whatever Charles may have told you." She has a slight twang, possibly from having grown up in Georgia or somewhere near there. "Boy, I am grateful you came by. I was gettin' a little stir crazy myself. Whattya say we head on up?"

She is fast-talking and charming and you instantly like her. She jangles the keys as she walks, and swings the door open with a flourish. "After you," she says, gesturing you in and up the stairs. You trudge up and say, "Thanks for letting me up here. I've always wanted to see the r—"

You don't finish your statement because you've pushed open the door and are staring at a bright red helicopter.

"Is this what he was talking about? Are you the pilot of this?" you say, amazed.

"Sure am," she says. "A fine piece of machinery, that." She strokes the side lovingly.

"Wow," is all you can master.

"You wanna sit in it?" Jenny says with unbridled enthusiasm. "It's pretty cool."

"Umm, yeah!" you say.

She unlocks the door and holds it open with the same flourish. "Hop on in! Just don't push any buttons or anything. We're not goin' anywhere just yet, and it takes me ages to reset the controls properly if they get out of order."

You swing yourself up into the cockpit on the passenger side. It's roomier than you'd expected, and you try on the noise-canceling headphones you find on the dash in front of you, just to complete the experience.

Because of these, you don't hear when Jenny slides open the other door and climbs in the back, so you don't have any time to hide the imaginary steering wheel you were using to pretend to fly the 'copter.

You're embarrassed, but Jenny graciously pretends not to notice.

"Ain't she great? Bell 407, excellent machine. Seats five people just as roomy as can be. Better than any other kind of travel," she says.

You twist around to look in the passenger compartment where she is sitting. There is room for three more people, and Jenny is lounging comfortably across the three black leather seats. There's even a cup holder!

"I never get to see it from back here," Jenny says. "Still love it, but I'll haveta ask you to put those headphones back and hop on out now."

"Wow, thanks, that was great," you say, jumping down to the rooftop and sliding the door closed. "I think I'm gonna have to get one of those."

"Oh, sure thing!" Jenny says, laughing and slapping you on the back.

Nothing could be better than sitting in that helicopter—except maybe flying it. "Hey Jenny?" you ask. "Why haven't you and Mr. Lee taken off yet? Why not just leave?"

"Ah, well the wind is too high right now. And besides," she says, "Mr. Lee don't want to. I don't decide, I just fly the sweetheart." She pats the machine lovingly and locks it up again.

"But if things keep proceedin' as they are, we might just havta leave this way," she adds.

"Oh yeah?" you ask. "What are you hearing?"

"Well it sounds plum crazy, but it's comin' from some pretty reputable sources," Jenny says. "The CDC says this disease, this—this whatever disease that's spreadin' like wildfire? They said on the news that it does somethin' to your brain. They said it makes you, like—well, like one of them zombies from old movies."

"Zombies?!" you ask, incredulous. "You can't be serious."

"'Fraid I am. That's why me and all Mr. Lee's people were starin' at the screen when you came up. It's pretty depressing, and it seems like no one knows just what to do right now." She turns and starts walking back down the stairs, and you follow her.

"Zombies?" You shake your head. "Real zombies?"

"Yeah." She says, suddenly somber. "Kinda a head trip, ain't it?"

You're back on Mr. Lee's floor.

Stunned with the one-two punch of discovering there is a helicopter on the top of your building the same day you discover New York is being taken over by zombies, you:

⊙ Follow Jenny to sit with the rest of Mr. Lee's employees. *Turn to page 93.*

⊙ Head back to your floor with the news. *Turn to page 54.*

The small metal table is cold, but at least you don't have to sit near other people. One of the upsides to New York is there is always someone to talk to; the downside is someone is always trying to talk to you when you couldn't give a damn.

You eat your salad, enjoying the sights and sounds of the city—okay, they might be slightly more panicky than usual—and are generally having a very pleasant lunch when you are accosted by a filthy person—you can't quite tell if it's a man or a woman under the immense coat and unruly hair—asking you for change.

Disgusted, you:

⊙ Ignore the request. It's your money, and you don't have to share. *Turn to page 68.*

⊙ Dig in your wallet for a few extra bucks. It's the fastest way to end an encounter with a panhandler. You know from experience. *Turn to page 69.*

There's barely enough room left at the counter, but you managed to squeeze in between a portly red-faced man eating a massive Philly cheesesteak and a subdued-looking Indian guy.

The blubbery fellow has apparently decided to chat up the whole deli, and he's barely chewing his food. Bits are falling out of his jowls. The man on your right looks so disgusted it seems he might vomit into his bowl of soup at any moment. He turns away, and the big guy turns his attention to you.

"I dunno what all de fuss is about," he's saying. "This is New Yoahk, we can handle anhthang, youknowwhattamean?"

You try to show the least interest possible, but he's elbowing you in the ribs.

"Mmm," you say, stuffing your mouth full of lettuce in a vain hope that he won't expect you to respond and he'll leave you alone.

"So a coupla folks got de sniffles, whattaIcare, ya kno? Ha, I member back when there was dat pig flu, you member that? All thos folks was walkin' around with face masks and shit, you kno?" He's elbowing you again. You just nod.

"They was talkin' like that was the worst, the fuckin' worst, but you kno what? I got that. I mean, yeah, I diddna feel so good for like, two days, but I'm a man, you kno, and I gotta do what I gotta do. I didn't even take one goddamn day offa work, because hard work, thas what this country is founded on." He says the last with a self-approving hearty laugh. You don't expect it when he slaps you on the back, and you nearly choke on a tomato.

"Hey, hey, sorry 'bout that," he says. "Dunno my own strength sometimes."

"Fine," you manage, your voice raspy. "I'm okay."

Without warning, the Indian man to your right suddenly does vomit into his soup, the half-eaten contents splattering on him, his bowl, the counter, and you. You step back from the counter, disgusted and alarmed, and the deli owner comes over with a towel.

"Hey, you okay?" he asks the man, who is moaning slightly. "It wasn't the soup, right? You were sick when you came in here, right?"

The man isn't saying anything, and the owner stands up and yells, "It wasn't the soup, keep eating!"

Everyone drops their utensils and heads for the door while the owner is distracted by the man, who is now heaving out an incredible amount of fluid considering he only ate half the soup.

You make it back to your office, and clean the soupy mess off your sleeve, but it's too late. About an hour later, you're not feeling too well.

You:

⊙ Try to find something, anything, in your office that might relieve your symptoms. *Turn to page 11.*

⊙ Go home early. This might get messy. *Turn to page 12.*

⊙ No time to leave; you're exhausted now. You curl up under your desk. *Turn to page 13.*

Y ou turn to walk away, but a gloved hand grabs your arm and pulls you back. The woman—because now that she's 4 inches from your face, you can see she's female under all the dirt—says, "Can't you spare any change?"

She has a really good grip on your arm, and a wild look in her eyes. You're about to answer when she begins coughing, huge wracking coughs full of phlegm, right in your face. Gross.

She's coughing pretty hard now, and has to let go of your arm to steady herself on the metal table. You back away, throwing some cash on the table—for her or the waitstaff, you don't particularly care—and head back to your office.

About an hour later, you're not feeling too great.

You:

⊙ Hunt for some medicine to make you feel better. Surely somewhere in this office there are some pills or something? *Turn to page 11.*

⊙ Sneak out and go home. You hate being at work when you're sick. *Turn to page 12.*

⊙ Decide it's too late; you curl up for a nap under your desk. Hopefully your boss won't come by to check on you like she did the last time. *Turn to page 13.*

You find a buck and some change, and you hand it to the person—probably female, maybe?—while managing not to touch her hand. So you're a little germaphobic, so what?

She doesn't even say 'thank you'; she just grunts and turns to talk to someone else. A moment later, you hear painful seal-like coughing. You turn to look and see the panhandler coughing in someone else's face. Man, that's gross.

You head back to your office, resolving to scrub extra-hard when you shower tonight. Bleah, germs.

After you've been at your desk awhile, you look up and realize most everyone else is away from their desks. Someone—Bruce from IT maybe?— is muttering loudly and typing fast.

You:

⊙ Find your coworkers, all standing and staring out of the windows down at the ground below. *Turn to page 19.*

⊙ Check in on Bruce. What's he so mad about? *Turn to page 20.*

Your sad replacement sandwich falls to the bottom of the vending machine, and you collect it with resignation. On the way back to your desk, you stop to get a glass of water from the workroom. Bruce, a well-muscled man who would be a better match for a sexy workout commercial than the IT department, is there, eating a pre-packed lunch. You were planning on eating at your desk, but you pull up a chair and join him.

"'Sup," he says.

"Just grabbing lunch," you say. "I can't believe the mayor says we're not supposed to leave the building."

In between mouthfuls of leftover spaghetti, Bruce says, "It sounds serious."

"Yeah, sure. Maybe next Godzilla will rise up out of the ocean, or we'll have a *Cloverfield* situation on our hands," you say sarcastically.

"It could happen," Bruce says. He's trying to sound intimidating and serious, but he's got marinara sauce on the corner of his mouth, so he looks like a toddler that tried to apply his mom's lipstick—except, you know, a burly middle-aged man instead. You can't help but smirk.

"Sure Bruce, whatever. You got your action plan all figured out?" you say. "I bet you do. You one of those survivalist man-versus-wild types?"

Bruce doesn't answer, which is answer enough in itself. His intent stare makes you a little uncomfortable. Maybe you should go back to your desk after all.

"Well I'll know who to talk to if it is Godzilla, anyway," you say, edging out of the chair and toward your desk. Talk about a lively lunch break. Geez.

You go back to your desk and play a couple of rounds of Angry Birds.

After awhile, you notice no one else is sitting at their desks; there seems to be a group clustered by the window. Bruce is the only one sitting at a desk, and the commotion over there sounds…intense.

You:

⊙ See what has halted the work day. Maybe something juicy has happened. *Turn to page 19.*

⊙ Check in on Bruce. What's happened now? *Turn to page 20.*

You probably should have learned to take the news seriously at some point, at least. To be fair, it was hard to think the news of the world was serious when it was delivered by a wise-cracking comedian, but maybe you could have tried harder.

Today though, it's pretty freakin' serious. The news of the infection or whatever—officials with important-sounding titles don't quite seem to know what was going on, or minor details like whether the effects were even caused by a disease or not—had only arrived in the city yesterday. By mid-morning, the infection was unstoppable. The people wandering the street? Probably infected already. Hard to tell until they were clinically dead (which was somehow different than actually dead, but just how was a little unclear) and they got up and tried to bite your face off. Which they were now doing. In numbers.

You lean back in your computer chair, tenting your fingers. So, to recap: This morning, totally normal. Afternoon, trapped in your office building. Outside, actual freakin' zombies.

You perform a literal facepalm, smacking yourself lightly in the face with your open palm. Holy cow.

Of all the places to have to deal with a zombie invasion, you are stuck at an office building? This wasn't covered in any of the zombie flicks you'd seen.

What does one do in this kind of situation? You think for a few minutes, but nothing good comes to mind.

You Google "office zombie invasion how-to."

The first couple articles suggest you "interview the candidate" and "temp to hire." Yeah, no, that's not the right kind of zombie. Even the internet isn't prepared for this. Even the CDC was unprepared, and they had released a full "how to survive a zombie invasion" press kit. You're pretty disappointed when you discover it isn't really good on specifics, and it's a little late now to stock up on canned goods.

Twitter is no help either. After searching the hashtag #NYCzombies, you discover that the rest of the country has declared the city off-limits. The army is setting up a blockade. There are rumors of air-drops being planned.

You're starting to feel pretty helpless. And then, the power shuts off.

It turns out office buildings are really dark without electricity. You can't so much as see the hand in front of your face.

Your smartphone still has about three-quarters of a battery left, and you fumble with it to turn on the flashlight app.

You:

     ⊙ Go huddle with your coworkers near the window, where it's a little brighter. *Turn to page 94.*

     ⊙ Warily head for the stairs. *Turn to page 95.*

     ⊙ Start crying for your mommy. *Turn to page 97.*

Sometimes when you're feeling sickly, it's mostly just because you're tired of work and being trapped indoors so much, so you figure a walk won't be too terrible.

You start moving in the direction of your apartment, just over two miles away. At first you're focusing on putting one foot in front of the other, but after a few minutes you feel a bit better and start to look around, take in the views.

There seem to be a lot of people out walking; particularly when you factor in the warning to stay inside. Traffic is fairly slow, but that's typical. What's a little unusual is how slowly the people around you are walking. Normally New Yorkers are constantly speed-walking from place to place, always moving like there is somewhere important to be. Today, however, the pace has slowed to a lackadaisical stroll.

It's almost…unsettling.

Your stomach takes another lurch, and suddenly you feel as if you've taken a dive on a rollercoaster.

You:

⊙ Keep walking. It's just one foot in front of the other. You can take it. *Turn to page 76.*

⊙ Hail a cab. Maybe walking wasn't such a great idea. *Turn to page 74.*

⊙ Head for the subway. *Turn to page 75.*

Clutching your stomach, you step into the street and flail an arm. Two cabbies pass you by, and you glare at them, quietly seething. The third stops, and you gratefully heave yourself in. You give the driver, a light-skinned black guy with a full beard, your address.

"And hurry, if you can," you squeak out. Your stomach rolls again as he pulls away from the curb.

"You don't look so good," he says, glancing back at you in the mirror.

Speak for yourself, you think, but you say, "Don't feel so hot. Going home."

He drives in silence for a few seconds, and you rest your throbbing head against the cool glass.

"You don't got that sickness the mayor was talkin' about?" he finally asks. There's a hint of a threat in his voice.

"No," you snarl, derisively. "I've just got food poisoning or something. I'll be fine." You're feeling a little defensive.

"Okay, okay," the cabbie says, then slides the plastic guard window shut. As it grates against its housing, you glare at the cabbie again. What exactly is he assuming?

You don't have time to find out, because he has arrived at your apartment building. You pay him, leaving off the tip just to piss him off, and climb the stairs to your fifth-floor walkup on wobbly legs. On days like this, you really hate your apartment.

You make it into your place, not even bothering to lock the door, and run to the bathroom.

You're in there for a while. It's pretty nasty.

You:

⊙ Collapse on your bed. Hopefully sleep will fix whatever is ailing you. *Turn to page 77.*

⊙ Make yourself a bowl of chicken noodle soup. *Turn to page 79.*

⊙ Check your symptoms on the internet. It's good to be informed. *Turn to page 80.*

For a weekday afternoon, the subway platform is particularly busy, full of blank-faced drones waiting to board the train to their destination. You don't take particular notice; you shove your hands in your pockets and stare straight ahead at the tracks, just like everyone else.

Because it's so busy, when the train arrives a moment later and a handful of people disperse down the exit, you are smushed into the car with the crowd, and find yourself haplessly dangling from one of the tethers in the ceiling, though the press of bodies around you could likely keep you standing even if there was a crash.

It's a short ride, but you're feeling claustrophobic by the time you get to your stop. You barely make it out at your exit, and tumble out of the subway car, stumbling at the edge. You need air after being so cramped in that car, and you lean against the nearest wall, your breathing strained. You slap your hand down squarely on top of a newly deposited piece of chewed bubble gum—probably spearmint from the smell on your hands. It's still slimy, and you spend the short walk back to your apartment trying to wipe the residue off your hands. That certainly doesn't make you feel any better. You're still trying to remove the slime as you enter your apartment and head straight to the kitchen sink to scrub the gum off.

You're still not feeling too well, so you:

⊙ Go lay down. You love naps. *Turn to page 77.*

⊙ Dig in the pantry for a can of chicken noodle soup. *Turn to page 79.*

⊙ Decide to research what might be causing your symptoms. *Turn to page 80.*

Y ou keep walking. It's not too much farther.

The pain in your head becomes more intense, and you lean against the brick wall of the nearest building to steady yourself. After a moment, you stagger on, only to be blinded by the migraine's—for that's what this stupid headache has clearly become—glowing aura. You blink your eyes hard against the painful flashes of color, to no avail, of course—the problem isn't your eyes, it's your head. You pause again, taking a few steadying breaths. Just a little…bit…farther.

You are less than 20 feet from the door to your apartment, but you've got to cross the street. You step out into the road, still half-blind—and are struck by a yellow taxi.

As you collapse to the pavement, you wonder if this is the taxi that might have dropped you off, had you just hailed one earlier. The thought slips from your head, and you lose consciousness. You don't wake up again.

TURN TO SECTION Z
Page 181.

Y ou fall into bed, not so much as bothering to pull back the covers or undress. Ugh. You feel miserable. You eventually get comfortable by pulling your knees all the way up to your chest in the fetal position and tucking your head under a pillow.

Hours later, you're still lying in the same twisted position when you wake up. It's dark, and… you hear a sound. It's a sort of shuffling. And it's coming from the end of your bed.

A moment later, there's a thump as something—someone?!—walks into your dresser. You hear a low moaning, and at first think it's coming from you—you're still not feeling well—but then realize that someone is in your room, moaning.

You turn on your bedside lamp. It's Mrs. Goldstein, your neighbor from down the hall. She's still wearing her white old-lady nightgown, and her lavender robe is hanging loose and open around her shoulders.

"Mrs. Goldstein, are you all right?"

Mrs. Goldstein turns to face you. Her head lolls on her shoulders oddly. She moans.

"Mrs. Goldstein, do you need me to call 9-1-1?"

The small Jewish woman is shuffle-stepping toward your bed in her aged house shoes. You think maybe she's having a stroke, and you reach up to grab her shoulder. Looking into her eyes, you say, "Mrs. Goldstein?" one more time.

For the first time, she seems to see you. She crumples forward into you, catching you by surprise. As you're trying to lift her off of you, you feel an odd sensation on your neck. After a moment, you realize it is her denture-less gums, chewing—or sucking—on you.

"What the f—!!" You try to push her away, but you can't even finish your statement before she pushes harder against you, her gumming mouth breaking the skin. Your neck bleeds.

You shove her away, knocking her back against the closet doors harder than you should hit an old lady, and hold a hand to your neck. Despite her lack of teeth, she got a pretty good bite in. Trying to stem the bleeding, you walk to the bathroom.

You're holding a towel to your neck when she arrives at the bathroom door. Her right arm is at an odd angle.

"Mrs. Goldstein, I'm sorry I shoved you, but…"

Mrs. Goldstein is not listening to you. She grabs your arm, and her frail hands have more strength than you'd have guessed, and bites your wrist. It bleeds in earnest.

You try to fight her off, but now you're bleeding from two wounds and you can't stop the flow in both at once. You slip on the bathroom mat and fall into the tub, hitting your head against the showerhead as you fall.

Great. Now you're bleeding in three places, and your neck is killing you.

On second thought, no, it's not your neck that's killing you—it's Mrs. Goldstein.

TURN TO SECTION Z
Page 181.

Chicken noodle soup can fix just about any ailment. It's a pantry staple. But you're not always super at buying groceries ahead of time, and it takes a few minutes of digging before you find a can, deep in the shadows of the farthest back corner of the pantry. The can is a bit dented and past its expiration date—you really need to clean out your kitchen more often, or at least donate some of these cans to charity or something—but when you open the can you decide it's probably still edible. I mean, it looks fine, so it's okay, right?

You plunk the noodles and broth into a bowl and heat it in the microwave. Before it's spun more than a few turns, the aroma wafts to your nostrils and your stomach starts to growl. There's nothing like a good bowl of chicken noodle soup, and you gulp it down before the bowl is even cooled.

But…it wasn't such a good bowl of chicken noodle soup. Maybe next time you should follow those expiration warnings. In the next hour or so, your headache and stomachache do feel much better, and you spend the rest of your day watching trashy TV and surfing Pinterest. But …then you wake up in the middle of the night. It starts with severe cramps, and soon you're hugging the porcelain god, begging for mercy as you puke what feels like your entire guts out. Then your vision gets blurry, and your face gets numb. You try to call 9-1-1, but you get a busy signal and your call never goes through. Your mouth goes dry—almost a relief after the vomiting— and you're so dehydrated you're having trouble getting off the floor, much less making any other calls. It takes a little while, but between the paralysis caused by the botulism and the dehydration, it's curtains for you. At least you won't have too many wrinkles.

TURN TO SECTION Z
Page 181.

This is the kind of crisis the internet was made for. You grab your laptop and click over to your favorite search engine. You type "symptoms: nausea, headache" into the search bar. Judging by the results, you might have a brain aneurism, a stroke, aseptic meningitis, a sunburn, or a migraine. Since you've been inside for most of the past two weeks, you're reasonably certain it's not a sunburn. Here's hopin' it's a migraine!

Oh, and there's a possibility that it's the new disease the mayor has been warning everyone about. Great. One more worry.

You regret searching for your symptoms now. Plus you're worried that there's some blood vessel in your head about to burst at any second.

There's not much else to do but call your best friend.

"I'm probably dying," you say when Adam picks up.

"That right?" he says, totally deadpan. That's the best thing about Adam; he totally gets you.

"Yup. I have a headache and a stomachache and I searched on the internet and the internet says I'm dying." You match his tone. It helps to joke about it.

"Can I have your stuff?" he says. "Do you have enough time to write up a quick will to ensure I don't have to go through any of that legal drama when I come to collect your stuff?"

"You're so materialistic. I call you, tell you I'm probably dying and you're my last phone call before I leave this metaphorical life sentence and all you care about is getting my flat screen TV and my collection of owl pellets," you say, lounging in your overstuffed couch.

"You know how I love owl pellets," he responds, just as dryly. "So what's really up?" he asks. You can hear him typing or something in the background, still trying to work despite your distraction.

"Wasn't feeling well, so I went home sick," you say, trying to be casual, trying not to think about the possibility of your imminent demise.

"Despite the mayor's warning?" he asks, only half-listening to you.

"Because of the mayor's warning," you say. "Seriously, can you imagine being trapped in a building with those people I call coworkers? Ugh. That's a certain level of hell, that's for sure."

"I can see that," he says. "Just another good reason I work from home. That and I don't like people much."

"Hey," you ask, trying to be casual, as if the thought only just occurred to you, "have you heard much about this disease the mayor's going on about?"

"Just snippets, but it sounds like things are getting worse out there. Hope you've got your groceries," he says.

"Now that you mention it, I could use some food," you say.

"Or you could come over here and hang," Adam offers. Offering to let you be near him when there's a chance you've got a horrible life-ending disease—that's a true friend.

You:

⊙ Hang up and head to the grocery store to stock up. *Turn to page 83.*

⊙ Go to Adam's apartment, a few buildings over. *Turn to page 84.*

⊙ Still aren't feeling too well, so you say "thanks but not now," and go take a nap. *Turn to page 77.*

That's it, you've had enough. You gather up your things and head for the door.

Alyssa mumbles something indeterminable as you walk by—sort of a muffled moan—but you just say, "I'm done here. See ya!" and walk on by without stopping.

When you hit the lobby, you see the security guard locking the doors. Damn it. You turn right, go past the bathrooms and down a hallway, and find the discrete side door the smokers frequent. It's still unlocked. You open the door—it still smells like stale smoke out here, gross—and head to the street.

Traffic is at a complete standstill. No way you can get a cab here.

You roll your eyes—New York City at its finest—and walk home.

An unusual number of people are out walking today. Huh. Maybe traffic is bad all over the city?

At any rate, you don't feel like talking, so you avoid eye contact with everyone around you, and circle wide whenever someone is on the same sidewalk as you. At least with traffic at a dead halt you aren't likely to get run over if you walk in the street.

A panhandler outside of your apartment moans as you walk by, trying to get your attention. "Get a job," you snarl, pushing past him when he reaches toward you. "I earned my money!"

You slam the door in his face, and he scratches at it pathetically as you climb the stairs to your apartment. You drop your stuff just inside the door.

After a few minutes at home, you decide to:

⊙ Go pick up groceries. *Turn to page 83.*

⊙ Go visit your best friend, Adam, who lives a few blocks over. *Turn to page 84.*

⊙ Go to Central Park. It's a nice day. *Turn to page 136.*

The last time you opened your fridge all you had was a bit of curdled milk and some takeout from several nights before. If you're going to be stuck in your apartment, you might as well have something to eat.

You leave your apartment and begin the walk to the market a block away, dodging other pedestrians and an errant bicycle messenger. Traffic has slowed down; maybe more people are heeding the mayor's warning. That's great for you; it'll make it that much easier to shop without having to jostle other customers for the peanut butter.

The market is owned by Mr. and Mrs. Chow, whom you recognize even though you haven't exactly been a frequent customer, so you say hello to the well-kempt man in the apron as you pass him. Just as you suspected, the market is reasonably empty. Perfect. You grab a basket and begin walking through the low-slung aisles. You get a couple of apples, two bags of chips, a dozen cans of soup—making your basket so heavy you switch to a small cart instead, no use breaking your arm—a few boxes of health bars, and, after a moment's consideration, a couple of bottles of water. You fill what's left of space in the cart with beer.

In the checkout lane, you hesitate in front of the selection of candy.

You decide you deserve a little pick-me-up, and grab:

⊙ a pack of gum. *Turn to page 86.*

⊙ a chocolate bar. *Turn to page 87.*

You grab your wallet and a light jacket and head out, locking the door behind you. Not many people are out, and you pass a man lying prone on the sidewalk. You're too busy muttering about homeless people needing to sleep somewhere besides the damned pavement to notice the bloodstains.

Adam's brownstone is only a block and a half away, but it might as well be a whole 'nother city. The tree-lined walkway creates cool shadows on the sidewalk, and there's less traffic here. You leap the few steps in a long stride and knock, rat-at-tat, at the glass-paneled door.

While you wait for your best friend to answer, you get the creeping tickling sensation at the back of your neck that you're being followed. You look around uneasily behind you, but all you can see is a small cluster of old ladies, shuffling their feet and walking awkwardly up the road.

Still, you're relieved when Adam opens the door.

"Hey, come on in," he says, closing and locking the door behind you. "Grab a drink and hang out. I'll finish what I'm working on in just a sec."

The nice thing about your best friend living nearby and working from home is that it's almost always okay for you to drop by at a moment's notice. The bad thing about your best friend working from home is he's always working.

You go to the fridge, help yourself to a beer, and stretch out on the couch.

"So, how's your day been?" you ask him.

"Eh, you know, the usual crap. Just gimmie one more second, I swear," he calls back from the other room. Yeah, you've heard that before. You turn on the TV and let your brain wallow around in the TruLife Story of a woman who was on disability because she couldn't work—she qualified because she had grown her fingernails (and toenails!) out so she could win a world record. The nails were several feet long, she was confined to a specially-made bed, and someone had to feed her and help her on the toilet.

Man, you really did pick the wrong line of work. If you could go back and do your third-grade career day all over again, you'd choose something like that, where you could sit around all day and be taken care of.

Your indolent reverie is broken by a knock at the door—Thump thump thump.

"Can you get that?" Adam calls. "I'll be right there, just…"

"Yeah, yeah, don't worry about it," you call back.

I guess the upside of letting you hang out at his place is Adam gets his very own butler. He lives in a nice neighborhood, but not that nice.

You can see the silhouettes of several people outside the frosted glass of the door—it's a bit early in the year for carolers. There's a thump thump at the door again.

"I'm coming already, geeze," you say.

Without bothering to look out the peephole, you turn the lock and open the door.

The old women you saw earlier are standing outside, swaying on their feet. Now that they're in front of you, you can see they aren't actually old. Well, one of them is, but the other two are considerably younger. The one on the far right is downright youthful—but you couldn't tell from their hunched and bedraggled appearance (just about every woman seems to be dyeing her hair nowadays).

The middle woman moans and lurches toward you, and you can see something is most definitely not right. "Hey, I didn't invite you in," you say, and try to close the door on her.

She doesn't even stop, and her wrist is caught in the door jam.

"Sorry 'bout that," you say, opening the door to free her again, "but really, you can't come in, I don't care what you wa—"

The motion of reaching for the door must have brushed back the woman's hair, because now you can see that a jagged round section of her throat is missing, like it was bitten off. She also shares an empty-eyed gaze with her two companions. All three are moaning quietly and shuffling their feet. The oldest seems to be having trouble holding her head up.

They each reach for you and push against the door. It is only with effort that you can hold the door mostly closed, but several hands come through the crack and claw at you.

You:

⊙ Apologize for hurting the ladies and let them in. They clearly need some kind of medical attention. *Turn to page 104.*

⊙ Holler for Adam. *Turn to page 106.*

⊙ Shove against the door with all your might. *Turn to page 108.*

As you reach out to grab your favorite brand of minty-freshness, you see movement out of the corner of your eye. Someone is just behind you.

It's a good thing the pack of gum is on the top shelf. If it had been any lower, you wouldn't have been able to react as quickly when Mr. Chow lunged for your head. You were in such a rush on the way in that you didn't notice the slack blankness in his face, but you do now, considering his face is only about 8 inches from yours as you scramble to hold him back with one arm. His eyes are open, but there is an emptiness to them that is deeply unsettling. As he windmills his arms, leaning forward against your restraining outstretched arm and working his jaw as if he intends to gnaw on your face, you shove him slightly backward, then run forward as fast as you can, pushing the laden cart in front of you. Mr. Chow is thrown off balance, and he staggers slightly to the right, careening into the stand full of candy. You don't look back, but push your groceries out the automatic door. You don't stop running until you get back to your apartment. What the hell?!

You:

⊙ Call 9-1-1. *Turn to page 88.*

⊙ Barricade yourself into your apartment. *Turn to page 89.*

Y ou really should have paid closer attention when you entered the store. Then maybe you would have noticed that Mr. Chow wasn't doing anything, didn't greet you like normal, didn't even look up. Then maybe when he snuck up behind you and grabbed you, you would have been ready.

But you weren't.

The chocolate bar you wanted was on the lowest shelf, and when you are crouched down to grab it, Mr. Chow appears behind you. He moans softly, and you look up, giving his claw-like hands a hand-hold on your ear and the collar of your shirt. He has a really good grip, and you try to pull away, but the way you are crouched is awkward and you stumble back. Mr. Chow's momentum carries him forward, and he lands on top of you. He never looked like he weighed too much, but when his full weight hits you it's enough to drive you back hard against the worn linoleum floor.

He's strong, and apparently motivated to get you, but seems uncoordinated, and you are able to push him off. You abandon your cart and start to run for the door. You're nearly there before you notice that Mrs. Chow is in your way. You start yelling that something is wrong with Mr. Chow, and run toward her without slowing—until you notice that she has the same slack-jawed look as Mr. Chow. Your yelling has attracted her attention, and now she, too, is moving toward you, hands outstretched. You try to back up, and slam right into Mr. Chow, who closes his arms around your neck in a chokehold and leans back so you both fall. While you struggle to get back up, Mr. Chow leans down and bites your cheek. You scream out and try to pull away, feeling blood rush down your face, but then Mrs. Chow is on top of you, making you the meat in a bizarre murderous sandwich. Before long, you are what's for dinner.

TURN TO SECTION Z
Page 181.

You dial the three numbers you memorized when you were about two years old, your hands shaking: 9-1-1.

The phone rings.

It rings again.

It rings.

You hear a three-tone cadence, then a mechanized voice says: "I'm sorry. All lines are currently busy. Please call back with your emergency at a later time."

Then the line goes dead.

What the hell?! Emergency lines aren't supposed to be busy, especially in a city as hectic and big as New York! There have to be thousands of operators.

Operators: maybe that will work. You dial "0" and listen intently.

Another automated message, another fake female voice. "All lines are busy. If you have an emergency, please call 9-1-1."

"I DID CALL 9-1-1," you shout into the receiver.

Okay, this is pretty scary now. What is going on?

You:

⊙ Barricade yourself into your apartment. *Turn to page 89.*

⊙ Go to Adam's. He'll know what's going on. *Turn to page 84.*

Something clearly wrong is going on outside, and you know what? You don't want any part of it.

You lock the deadbolt on your apartment, then the smaller lock in the doorknob. You stare at the door for a moment, then rush off to the closet. You return with a shabby toolbox and a handful of screws.

Crazy monsters are not getting in HERE. No way.

You realize you don't have anything to nail to the door, and besides, it's metal. After a moment's hesitation, you gently lift your flat screen TV off its stand and then shove the heavy piece of furniture in front of the door. It's going to be a little harder to pick out your favorite movie now, but that should slow anyone down.

Except—except if they come in the fire escape.

You run to your bedroom and lean out the window. You used to sit out there, in your first days of the apartment, but eventually you put your hand in enough pigeon crap that you decided the bohemian thing wasn't for you.

You decide you're probably safe from the fire escape route, as the ladder doesn't quite go all the way to the ground. But someone could still come in from above—after a moment's hesitation, you decide to clear the table in front of the window. It's more likely that you are going to need an escape route than a zombie—because that pretty much seems like what is going on out there—is going to come in; they aren't exactly known for being graceful.

You are a-jitter with nervous energy. What else do you need to do? You dive into your closet and pull out every candle you have, arranging them sporadically around your apartment—it's not too hard; it's not a very big place.

Matches! Do you even have any?

More digging reveals a lighter and half a box of strike-on-box matches, as well as seven lightly used birthday candles. You put those where you can find them easily; you don't know what you might need.

After that, there's not much else you can do.

You:

⊙ Take a nap. All that work really wore you out. *Turn to page 77.*

⊙ Turn on the news. *Turn to page 153.*

⊙ Call your best friend. *Turn to page 154.*

Y ou came all this way, so you feel obligated to at least look at the rest of the roof, though you keep throwing sidelong glances at the helicopter, imagining yourself at the controls. You wonder momentarily if everyone in a helicopter has to talk in that helicopter voice you always hear from the traffic radio DJs—'uh, roger, Johnny, there's a big wreck on the southbound lane,' with a rhythm of thudding rotors in the background.

What a jerk, that guy, not letting you even sit in his helicopter. Mr. Lee has strolled leisurely to the far edge of the roof, and is peering down meditatively. You vindictively walk the other way. Some company he turned out to be.

The roof is flat, except for some artificial texturing that crunches under your feet, with a slight edge all the way around—the kind that a flying superhero might grab onto to prevent a fall in the climactic scene of a movie. There is the water tower, and a set of four industrial air conditioners. There is a much taller building to your right, looking so close that maybe you could touch it if you leaned over far enough, and an open street adjacent. That was where the commotion was coming from earlier. You stand a few feet away from the edge and try to look over. You get a sense that traffic is nearly a standstill, but there seem to be people moving down there.

"See anything interesting?" Mr. Lee calls.

You shake your head. "I mean, I can't tell what I'm looking at from up here anyway," you say.

"There does seem to be something going on a bit to the south of here," Mr. Lee says, pointing. You walk a little closer, still well back from the edge, but it's hard to see much of anything. There are a few police cars, lights flashing, but the doors are open, and people are walking by in small groups.

You:

⊙ Step up to the edge to try to get a better look. *Turn to page 92.*

⊙ Go back inside. The roof—aside from the helicopter, of course— wasn't that interesting after all. *Turn to page 91.*

"Well, thanks anyway, Mr. Lee," you say, walking back toward the building.

Mr. Lee says nothing.

"I guess I didn't realize how short our building was compared to some of the others." Ever since you were a kid, you haven't been able to shut up. You hate awkward silences. Every mote of your being insists you've got to keep jabbering. "But a helicopter! Wow-ee! I sure wish I could have one of those. I'll have to get one, you know, if we survive this, ha-ha. Say, Mr. Lee, what would it take to get a seat on that thing if you decide to ride out?"

Mr. Lee stares at you steadily. "That's not a price you could ever afford." There's no trace of malice in the statement; it's just completely deadpan—no feeling at all.

"Huh. Well that's too bad for me, I guess. I've always wanted to ride a helicopter. Guess today's just not my day." You throw him a smile you hope is earnest and good-natured. It's a bit strained.

Mr. Lee locks the door to the roof behind you; it's like he thinks you might try to go back up there and mess with his helicopter (you totally were planning to go back and mess with his helicopter).

Pretending to be offended, you huffily:

⊙ Decide to hang out with Mr. Lee's employees for awhile. They've got a really nice big screen up here. *Turn to page 93.*

⊙ Head home. Forget this place. *Turn to page 82.*

⊙ Check back in with your coworkers. *Turn to page 54.*

You're curious. That's really all there is to it. So you take a step closer, and lean over.

Then you take another step closer, and lean over.

"Watch your footing, there," Mr. Lee says. "There seems to be some fresh—"

You don't hear the last part of what Mr. Lee said, but you have the time to figure out it must have been "pigeon droppings" or something equally eloquent but still meaning "slippery bird shit," after you slip on the substance and tumble over the edge of the building. You can see, as you fall facing up at Mr. Lee, that he was at least kind enough to try to grab you, but you were too far away and fell too fast.

The only good news, for you, is that not even enough of you remains intact after a 40-story drop to interest the mulling mindless masses below. You smash into the concrete sidewalk, neatly crushing a recently undead individual. Your blood trickles into the storm drain and into the Hudson River.

THE END

You are more than happy to take a seat on the floor with Mr. Lee's employees. Their big-screen TV is top-of-the-line, LED flat screen, the works. It even has some sort of backlighting, which would be cool if it were showing something other than gory images of the zombies invading the streets below. There also seem to be refreshments around here somewhere, because several people have drinks they are ignoring. One guy has a cookie. You'll have to find one of those, definitely.

"Excuse me," you say, "may I sit here?"

You hear a quiet "yes," and look into the eyes of

⊙ The most beautiful woman you have ever seen. *Turn to page 155.*

⊙ A man handsomer than your wildest imaginings. *Turn to page 157.*

⊙ Both an incredibly attractive man AND, amazingly, a gorgeous woman. (You've always been good at multitasking.) *Turn to page 159.*

You go to stand next to the window, where you see a few other silhouettes against the grey backdrop of the sky.

"What do we do, what do we do?" Nick is shaking so much you think you can hear his knees rattling.

"I DON'T WANNA DIE," Kristina half-screams, hysterical.

Their fear is contagious. You start to shake. "It's so dark. And no one is coming for us, no one! We're gonna be eaten alive in here!" you say, your voice going suddenly hoarse.

This is no good. You can't stay here with these people. You:

⊙ Head for the stairs. *Turn to page 95.*

⊙ Hide. *Turn to page 97.*

Okay, so you've kinda got a fear of the dark.

Whatever.

It's a totally rational fear.

Take now, for instance. You know the building is beset by monsters that want to eat you, and now it's dark and you can't even see them coming.

So you panic a little.

You've got your phone and the little flashlight app, at least.

You start walking for the stairs, which you know are somewhere to your right. You feel your way along, shaking the walls of cubicles as you go.

Someone behind you calls your name, but you've reached the stairs. You're committed. You're getting outta here. You fumble for the cold metal handle and pull the door open.

The stairwell is inky blackness darker than anything you've ever imagined.

Trembling, you step forward, feeling forward with your toes before you take a step. Your phone leaves a ghoulish light, but the dark seems like it will swallow you up. You know there is a landing before the stairs, but you can't guess where it might end. You step forward, cautious. Step by step, you guide yourself down.

You've gone down two flights when your cell phone goes suddenly dark. You yelp and fumble with it, desperate to turn it back on, and it slips from your hands and falls with a clatter.

Oh god.

The dark eats you up.

Now you're alone, in darkness so dark it's palpable. The darkness is like a living thing, climbing into your mouth and eyes, suffocating you with its tentacles. You're floating in a never-ending sea of darkness. No, worse: you're trapped on a stairwell.

You scrunch your eyes all the way closed and inch forward.

You find the first step, grasp the handrail with both white-knuckled hands, and continue your slow, anxious descent.

After a few steps, you begin to hyperventilate, and the room spins, even though when you open your eyes you can't see any room at all. You slump down, resting your head against the cool wall.

You start to cry.

You don't know how long it is—hours, minutes?—before you hear the sounds, sounds that haunted your nightmares as a kid when you were sure there were monsters under the bed. Shuffling noises, and low Jacob-Marley moans.

You sob harder and begin to rock yourself. "Ohpleaseohplease ohpleaseohplease aghhh ahhhh," you sob.

The noises get closer, louder, steadily rising up from below.

You start to crawl back up the stairs, but you are exhausted with fear and, any way, it seems impossible.

The monsters from under the bed are finally going to get you.

There is nothing you can do to stop them.

You've been so naughty.

You sob louder.

Tight fingers wrap around your ankle.

Your screams echo in the stairwell, sending chills through listeners on every floor.

TURN TO SECTION Z
Page 181.

Today has been, like, a really hard day, and—even if you've never told anybody since you were 4 years old—you're afraid of the dark. And it's really, really dark. It's just too much. You start to cry, big sniffily hiccupy crocodile tears. You ball your fists and pull your hair. It's just all so unfair! This was totally not supposed to happen; it is especially not supposed to happen to you. Why did the zombie invasion have to happen to you?!?

You scrunch up into the smallest space possible; you start by pulling your feet up into your chair and squishing yourself into a ball, but that gets really uncomfortable after a few minutes, so you get up, push your chair away angrily for being such a jerk, and crawl under your desk. It's darker under there, but you imagine it's a bit like a nice cave, and you feel safe. You lean into a corner and let the tears fall.

You can't maintain the hysterics for long, and your cries subside to mere sniffles. You hug your knees. You can no longer hear your coworkers moving or talking. You think maybe they forgot about you. That would be so typical for the way today has gone. They're jerks, too.

You stay there, in the dark, feeling sorry for yourself and rocking gently back and forth, for a long while.

Suddenly you hear a loud THUMP followed by "oof," like someone walked into a cubical wall or desk.

You:

⊙ Call out "Hello?" *Turn to page 98.*

⊙ Crawl out from your hiding place. *Turn to page 100.*

⊙ Do nothing. *Turn to page 102.*

The footsteps stop after you call out, but there is no other reaction, no indication of who or what is out there, so you try again: "Who's there?"

You climb out of your hiding place and feel around for something to arm yourself with. You end up with a weighted tape dispenser and a stapler. It's a start, at least.

You call out: "Hey! Who's there?" as loud as you are able. Your voice hangs in the dark of the office.

The shuffling steps come closer, a drag-step, drag-step, and beneath that, a kind of whuffing breathing sound, like a big dog panting. You heft your tape dispenser in one hand, ready to throw it as soon as you see something.

You wait, listening to the beating of your heart and the drag-step drag-step drag-step. It seems to be coming closer, but you can't be sure how close it is in the dark maze of the cubicles. You take a hesitant step forward, peering into the darkness.

All you can see in the dim light are the whites of someone's eyes, light grey against the black. Someone is coming closer, on your row. From the sound of the walk, they probably can't run. You might be able to run away.

You hesitate.

The shuffle-steps come closer. Two more shuffle-steps later, the building's barista, a shaggy-haired 20-year-old in a green apron, steps into the grayish light coming through the window. His skin is sallow, eyes empty, and his left foot is bent backward. He drags the twisted leg forward, and his knees buckle slightly under his weight, but he doesn't seem to notice. There is a dark fluid covering his white shirt. You have a feeling it isn't coffee.

All semblance of a plan leaves you, and you throw your tape dispenser at him, silently hoping he'll say "ow, that hurt!" when it strikes him. But he disappoints you and doesn't even flinch. The tape dispenser clips him in the shoulder, tumbling away uselessly. He doesn't even slow down.

You panic and run, stapler upheld, in the opposite direction. There's something deeply unsettling about the coffee boy, and your belly aches with fear. You stop in the shadows, your back against a filing cabinet, hoping zombies are something like T-Rex, that he won't see you if you don't move. Anyway, your knees are shaking, not really obeying your commands to run. You cling to your stapler like a three-year-old hugs his favorite teddy bear, and hear someone whining close by. You look around, but realize it's you making those whimpering noises. You fight the sudden irrational urge to staple your own mouth shut to make yourself stop.

Meanwhile, the barista is shuffling, shuffling. He rounds the corner of the cheap cubicle wall—and comes directly toward you.

"Eeeeehhhhhh," you whine, shaking fitfully, then run, not even looking where you're going. You only know you have to be not-here. Not here, anywhere else!

You crash hard into the corner of a desk, tearing your pants, but don't slow, just running, running, limping slightly now from the impact with the furniture. Your eyes aren't even open—not that it matters much, they were useless in the dark, but now they are closed not because of darkness but because of the fear rising in a thick bile up your throat. Your eyes are screwed so tight that, even if the room was lit, you wouldn't have seen the wall.

You run head-first into it, the impact sending a shockwave of pain, then numbness, down your spine. Your brain does the only sensible thing it can do and shuts off. You fall to the floor in a classic comedy pratfall.

It's impossible to know how long you were unconscious. You come to slowly, sound returning to your ears first. You're not sure if your eyes are open or closed; the view is blackness either way, isn't it? You try to open your eyes anyway; the room is wobbling underneath you, and pain blossoms up your neck. You wish you could have stayed unconscious. That really wasn't so bad.

The shuffling sound is back. It is close. It is louder. Now instead of two shuffling feet, there are many.

You try to will yourself to move, but nothing is happening. Disoriented, fatigued, and at least half-numb, you can do nothing but wait, the blood on your forehead slowly congealing.

You are still alive when they begin to eat you.

THE END

You crawl out from under the desk, self-consciously trying to wipe away the salt trails from your crying spree. Gah, you've probably got puffy eyes and everything…then you remember it's so dark that no one will see you anyway. Never mind.

You stretch your legs cautiously, trying to work out the kinks. Note to self: Don't cower under desks. It's bad for the circulation. You hear the muffled sound of a door closing in the distance, and you head toward it. You try to keep quiet, but you're reasonably sure zombies have bad coordination and wouldn't have made it up to your floor, so it's probably just one of your coworkers. Still, you'd rather be careful.

You reach the center wall in your office and feel along it for the door. There's the whiteboard, slightly visible even in the dark gloom, so about eight more feet and you should be at the door—there it is! You turn the handle and peer into the workroom. Even darker in there; no exterior lights. You fish out your smartphone again and shine its weak light around the workroom before you step in. In the drawer next to the sink are some mismatched steak knives that made their home in the office some years before. Community use. You think now is probably a good time to use them. You grab two, one for each fist. It's pretty awkward to hold both your phone and the knives, but you more or less manage. You head deeper into the center of the building. Just past the workroom is the hallway, and somewhere in there you should find the stairwell. That's the closest thing you've got to a plan.

It's a lot harder to aim your light now, so you walk uncertainly. You round a corner and nearly leap out of your skin when you see a light, but it's just the reflection of your phone in the vending machine window. Heart pounding, you pause and take a breath before continuing. That's when you hear it—shuffling steps somewhere behind you. Apparently you were wrong about zombies and stairs. You move a little faster, but the moaning is getting closer. You drop your phone, and the eerie white light illuminates the outline of a heavyset male zombie wearing a forest green apron. Great. You're going to get eaten by the barista.

He swipes at you, and you dodge under his arm and run for the stairs.

Without the light, you can't quite tell where they start, and you overstep just a little, your foot stepping out into nothing.

Maybe you would have been okay if you hadn't stopped to get the knives—badly bruised and beaten up from rolling down a flight of stairs, but okay. But you do have the knives, and when you roll, one jabs you in the side. Between your probably-broken bones and the slow-bleeding stomach wound, you're dead meat. Literally.

TURN TO SECTION Z
Page 181.

Hell no you're not going to get out of your hiding place now! That sound might be a zombie. Or a guy with a gun. Or Godzilla, for all you know.

Nope, you're staying riiiiiight here.

Just to be cautious, you put your hand across your mouth to muffle the sound of your breathing, and hope that these zombies aren't heat-seeking. Zombie-missiles. That's all you need.

The shuffle-step tread continues. Distantly, you hear a door creak open—probably the workroom door, that thing never did open quietly, so disruptive—and the sound of more footsteps. You stay where you are, barely breathing. You cover your eyes, just for good measure, but they were already wedged tight despite the dark.

More shuffling steps, then a low moan, like someone who lost a contact on the floor and has just realized there is no way they are going to find it so they'll have to go around half-blind the rest of the day. You open your eyes a crack. You can just make out the shape of two high-heeled feet pacing past your desk. One heel is higher than the other, maybe broken. That might explain the shuffle.

Classic movies say that zombies mostly react to movement. You're hoping that's true, and aren't feeling particularly keen to test the theory. You try to hold your breath but realize you're already holding it, so you have to release a burst of air before you can suck in another. It makes a whooshing sound...not particularly well muffled by your hand.

The heeled feet near your desk stop shuffling. Oh crap oh crap oh crap.

The squeaky door slams open—probably left a hole in the wall; the building's owner is gonna be so pissed—and someone with fast steps runs in, followed by more fast feet. You hear a whump followed by a dense-sounding thud, and the sound of office detritus being flung off a desk. High-heels goes shuffling in the direction of the disturbance.

That was a bit too close of a call, so you think maybe it's time to abandon your desk-cave. Your muscles ache from the position; how long were you under there anyway? You hobble a bit as you try to stand.

Your eyes have adjusted to the dark some—the scary, scary dark—and you can make out a few shapes darker against the darkness. Three shuffling forms, heads rolled to one side as if too heavy to hold up, grasping at two normal-looking forms. The taller has a long pole of some kind; by the clanging sound it's making as it strikes a zombie, it's metal.

Fighting zombies doesn't seem like it's really for you. You cautiously back away from the disturbance.

The larger form—is it...Bruce?—is swinging the pole like a club, keeping the shufflers out of arms' reach. The smaller form has long hair and you think it's maybe Becky. She seems to be good at using her environment; she just pushed a rolling desk chair into a zombie, shoving it back hard against the glass window in an echoing thud.

They've got this.

It's hard to tell in the dark, but you've worked in this office long enough to know the stairs are somewhere to your right. Feeling your way along, you start moving in that direction, away from the fight going on behind you. You flinch every time you hear one of those bone-cracking thuds.

The fight is over fairly quickly, and you hear voices—definitely Bruce and Becky—speaking in low tones.

You are nearly to the door when the metal club smashes into your skull. Apparently one of your coworkers, your supposed goddamn friends, mistook you for a zombie. You don't have much fight in you to begin with, but the heavy blow to the back of the head gets rid of whatever you might have had, and you crumple to the floor. As the blood flows out of your brain you think "I really shouldn't have come in to work today."

Bruce and Becky did the job right. You're definitely not coming back.

THE END

You start to shove the door closed, but then you remember that Adam lives in a nice part of town and these are probably his neighbors. You really shouldn't be rude to them.

You open the door. "I'm so sorry, ladies, you frightened me. I hope I didn't hurt you," you say, taking the older woman's hand in your own.

You bend over her arm, turning over her wrist—geeze, there's no need for her to resist this much, you're just trying to help!—to check for a break or a bruise, when one of them leans in and nips you on the ear. You slap a hand over your throbbing earlobe—crap, are you bleeding?!—and step back. "What the hell?!"

Those three witches are now all inside the house, shuffling blank-eyed toward you. "Adam, get out here already!" you yell.

You start to push the youngest woman away. She's the grabbiest, her nails digging in to your wrists.

Adam takes just about forever to come out of his study, but when he does, he reacts quickly. He assess the situation, grabs the coat rack, and steps in front of you to swing it—coats flying—at the crones. "Get. Out. Of. My. House," he says, punctuating each word with a jab from the mahogany coat rack. It takes a few minutes, but he forces them back outside, and you shove the door to with a panting sigh.

"Oh my god, man, thank you," you say, panting. The blood from your ear and the cuts in your wrist has started to flow in earnest. "Hey, you got a first aid kit or something?"

"Yeah," Adam says, rubbing his forehead. "What the hell was that?" he says, as he guides you toward the kitchen. Adam must be accustomed to a kitchen accident or two.

"I have no damn idea," you say. "You...you don't think they were the sick people we've been hearing about on the news, do you?"

Adam looks a bit pale, then tries to compose himself. "Nah, I bet they're just some weirdos tryin' to scare people." Adam has never been that great of a liar.

He bandages your wrist—it takes four Band-Aids—and tries to patch up your ear but the blood is keeping the adhesive from sticking, so after awhile you decide to let it be.

"You wanna just watch a movie or something?" Adam asks. He probably feels bad for making you answer the door and get bitten by crazy women.

"Yeah, that would be great," you say. You sit down to a re-watch of Casablanca.

Damn that movie is good.

But you don't even make it halfway through. While you watch, you feel woozy, and pass out for a few minutes.

Except you didn't pass out.

You died.

And when you come back as a horrible freak-against-nature monster, you eat your best friend. He's just sitting there, looking so delicious to your barely conscious zombie self. "Mmmmaahhhmm," you moan. At first, he just swats you away; he's too intent on the movie to notice. So you crept closer on the couch. Adam doesn't even turn around until you are there, hovering open-mouthed behind his shoulder.

He only has time to scream before you clamp down on his throat. You hit a major artery, and he bleeds out, spasming on his cream-colored carpet, as you slowly eat him alive.

Here's lookin' at you, kid.

TURN TO SECTION Z
Page 181.

"Adam! GET YOUR ASS OUT HERE WE'RE BEING ATTACKED!" you yell at the top of your lungs. You hear a clatter in the other room—he must have literally dropped everything he was doing—and Adam rounds the corner with a wiffle bat. His eyes go round when he sees you leaning with your back against the door, trying to hold back flailing well-manicured hands.

"What the hell?!" he says, walking closer.

"They just showed up and tried to get in," you say, panting. "Could you help me here?!"

Together you manage to close the door, Adam jabbing at the women with his red plastic bat when a hand reaches in too far. After locking it with the deadbolt and the lower lock, you both lean against the door, exhausted.

"Um," you say. "Maybe we should have paid more attention to the news."

Adam nods. You both get up and plunk in front of the 46-inch flat-screen TV.

After a pause, Adam says, "I think I'm just gonna go check the doors and windows," and gets up.

"You know, I think I will, too." You can still see the women outside, manicured nails scratching at the door. You shiver as you walk by.

You climb the stairs and verify that every window is closed, the shutters drawn tight, before you come back down.

Adam is standing in the middle of the living room, wielding a rusty Civil War-era sword held low.

"What the hell are you gonna do with that?" you say.

"I'm gonna protect us!" He sounds a little indignant.

"With that rusty thing? That couldn't cut through butter!" Seriously, that blade is as sharp as an anxious golfer's pencil.

Adam says nothing, but lays the antique saber across his knees reverently.

"I guess it is better than the wiffle bat," you say, and sit next to him on the couch.

He looks at you out of the corner of his eye, then leans forward and clicks on the television.

The signal comes in with a lot of interference.

"—Extreme. Danger." A frazzled newscaster is sitting behind her desk, looking pallid despite the layers of makeup. "This plague has been called 'unprecedented,' by hospital officials. If at all possible, do not leave your homes." The screen cuts out for a second, then blips back on. "The mayor's office has said they are deploying police officers. If you feel ill, it is essential that you isolate yourself from others—" the screen goes fuzzy for another half-second. "—And do not, repeat, do NOT go to the hospital."

The newscaster looks down and sniffles. The screen cuts to a scene of the sick people—zombies, let's just call them what they are—shuffling around a parking lot. Several are methodically thumping on a metal door. You can hear the sound of mucus rattling around the pretty anchor's nostrils; she's trying to hold back tears. With a ragged breath, she continues, "This is li-live footage from—from—from our parking lot. Just an hour ago, there were only"—there's a long phlegmy sniff—"there were only two." The newscaster breaks down into sobs. "You—you may recognize our Weatherman, Todd Waltson"—more ragged sniffles—"among the group. He-he-he went out to investigate for a live report, ladies and gentlemen, and was bitten."

Sure enough, there's the weatherman in his trademark bow tie. His jacket is torn—as is half his face—and he is slow-motion throwing himself against the building with the other monsters outside.

The screen cuts back to the haggard-looking newscaster. Tears are slicing rivets through her perfect makeup. "Based on this situation, we here at Channel 11 believe that the sickness is mostly transmitted via bodily f-f-fluids. We have not yet received con-confirmation from the CDC, but they do advise that everyone stay inside."

The station cuts to commercials. A cheerful cartoon bird tries to sell you wholly unhealthy cereal.

Adam mutes the TV.

"Well," he says. You stare at each other for a long minute. "Huh."

"Yeah," you say. You sink back into the couch. "Think this could all be some kind of *War of the Worlds* thing? Someone on Twitter got all excited, whipped up some imaginary frenzy?"

Adam turns to stare at the front door. The silhouettes of the three women are still there, swaying. Sometimes you can hear a low moan.

"Yeah," you say. "I guess it would have to be one helluva good story."

Adam runs a hand down his hair. "So what are we gonna do?"

"Well," you say, "why don't we...

⊙ ...fortify this place, you know, just in case?" *Turn to page 109.*

⊙ ...pop in a movie and hang out for awhile?" *Turn to page 112.*

⊙ ...get out there and put down some zombies?!" *Turn to page 114.*

You are so busy outright panicking that you are going to be eaten by three crazy women that you completely forget about Adam or anyone else in the world. Your whole universe has focused down to this door and keeping it closed, no matter what.

Keeping your left foot braced against the door, you lean far back to get some momentum, then throw yourself at the door as hard as you can.

The three wrists grasping at you through the doorway crunch—you're fairly sure that's the sound of bones snapping. But the hands continue to claw at you, and they don't bleed, though the lowermost one is now hanging at a disturbingly acute angle from its arm.

You feel a bit sick and turn back around. You brace your feet far in front of you and lean back with all your might.

The hand attached to the broken wrist pulls your hair.

You flinch away in reflexive terror and pull away. The attacking women reach in a little farther.

Desperate now, you repeat your back-then-forward-again lunge.

Outside, there's a low distressed moan. The broken hand falls off onto the tile floor of the entryway. It's still twitching. You vomit the entire contents of your stomach.

The sudden and painful compression of your stomach forces you away from the door, albeit only for a second. It's enough. You're holding your stricken stomach, kneeling over the pool of your partially-digested lunch, when the first woman comes in. She's the one now missing a hand.

"Adam!" you scream, eyes now bigger than the contents of your stomach. "OH MY GOD ADAM, HELP!" You slip on the greasy, bile-smelling debris, falling flat into it. You start to crawl forward, but the other women have now entered the house.

Adam is too late to save you. He watches in horror as you are eaten alive in his hallway, then runs screaming out the back door. Your last sight is of your best friend turning his back on you.

THE END

The zombies pounding on the front door manage to hit simultaneously, and the door rattles ominously on its hinges.

"You know, that seems like it's probably a good idea," Adam says, glancing sidelong at the shivering door.

Ever the info-geek, Adam peels off to Google "zombie preparedness" or something like that, and you head to the kitchen to account for your food stuffs.

Adam is a better shopper than you are, and he's got a decent bounty of canned foods, even if some of them are leftovers from two Thanksgivings ago. He also has a relatively new bag of oranges—only one has gone squishy and moldy—and a mountain of snack foods. You grab a pitcher and fill it with water, then hunt around in the cabinets for more water-storage containers. After some deliberation, you pour the not-quite-expired quart of milk into several glasses, rinse out the plastic jug, and refill it with water. You note with relief that there is still a good amount of beer.

You pop one open and are enjoying a long draw when Adam comes back. He's printed the CDC disaster preparedness guide. It's ten pages long.

"Seriously?" you ask. "Holy cow, we've got a lot of work to do."

Adam looks from the beer in your hand to the two small jugs of water. "We're going to need a lot more to drink," he says.

For the next hour, you and Adam stomp around the house gathering the items on the list and heaping them in a pile on the living room table. After a brief but intense debate, Adam leaves you to fill every available plastic or glass container with water, including a bucket that he usually used for mopping the floor. You make a mental note not to drink out of that one. Meanwhile, Adam fills the bathtub upstairs to the brim with water to be used for washing or, if push comes to shove, drinking.

You build a pyramid out of the canned foods, but you're feeling a lot more confident about the snack food. It's a good thing Adam has a serious junk food habit.

You're hunting for the flashlight, which Adam claims is in the hall closet, but you're not finding it and you're about to give up when the drumming on the door, constant for the past hour, ends with a loud CRACK. You and Adam both rush to the entryway. There is a long but thin crack down the side of the door, around the deadbolt mechanism.

"Shit, that's all we need now," you say.

"I think it's time we board up the doors and windows, dontcha think?" Adam says, already walking to the basement.

"Looks like it. Do you even have nails or anything like that?"

Adam isn't exactly the handy type.

"I don't know. Maybe a couple?" he says. "Hey, let's block the door in before we head downstairs."

A tall bookcase seems like the best candidate. It's too heavy to move while loaded, so you toss books and knickknacks to the floor to clear it out, then drag it in front of the door.

"Well, that should slow them down for a while," Adam says.

"But the door opens inward," you say. "Won't they just push it down?"

This clearly hadn't occurred to Adam, and he looks stunned. "Oh, shit, you're right. Let's get the La-Z-Boy."

Further lifting gets the plush leather chair propped up against the bookcase, theoretically making it harder for invaders to come in.

There are several windows on this floor, but most are up off the ground. The back door is the next threat. With you working as lookout, Adam runs outside and drags in his round metal grill, reasoning that if you can't use it defensively, maybe you can cook with it. That's also the reason he runs out a second time, for the charcoal and matches.

You suspect it is because he has an unhealthy attachment to that grill.

A rummage through the basement reveals only a handful of picture-hanging nails and some screws, but it's moot anyway, because Adam doesn't have a single stick of wood. You cover the kitchen window with cardboard and hope it gives passing zombies the impression that nobody is home. You barricade the back door with the desk from the entryway. It should keep the door closed, but it won't help if the glass breaks, so zombies will still be able to reach in. It's the best you can manage.

There is a loud ZAP followed by a BOOM that echoes across the buildings, and the power shuts off. Peering through the blinds in the front room, Adam says a transformer blew.

Finding that flashlight takes new importance. With the windows closed or card-boarded up, it is really dark. After several minutes of curses and thudding, Adam appears, the flashlight glowing a dull yellow.

Looks like the next thing you'll need to find is batteries.

Adam lights a few candles so you have enough light to work by, and you continue stacking your survival kit on the dining table. You find a radio, but you'll have to find more batteries for it, so you spend a half-hour taking apart every possibly battery-operated item in the house, including an RC car Adam claimed he was going to give to a nephew but never did. Suuuure, Adam, sure.

The stack has a first aid kit and extra Band-Aids, all the ibuprofen in the house (for once it's a good thing that Adam tends to buy in bulk), a hammer, the screws and nails, a Philips-head screwdriver, four rolls of toilet paper, one partially used roll of paper towels, all the blankets from the linen closet, all the towels except the one Adam used this morning because that one's still damp, duct tape, bleach (you're not sure what you might use that for, but it was on the list so Adam insists on putting it in the pile), and, though you almost forget, a manual can opener.

And you're exhausted.

"Can we take a break now?" you ask Adam.

"You think the doors are secure enough?" Adam is still worried.

"Sure, it's totally fine," you respond. "I'm tired. Can we go sleep for awhile? We're not going to do all that great fighting off the undead if we're practically dead on our feet as well."

"Fine," Adam says. "Fine, we can take a break."

You say:

⊙ "We can just sleep down here. We already have all the blankets." *Turn to page 126.*

⊙ "I want to sleep on a real bed. I'm going upstairs." *Turn to page 130.*

"I guess we might as well, since we aren't going anywhere else anytime soon," Adam says, kicking back in the couch.

"You got any beer or anything?" you ask. He nods, and you get two cold ones out of the fridge. You pop a bag of popcorn for good measure.

Adam is putting in the movie as you return, balancing the two bottles tangled between your fingers and the overflowing bowl of Extra-Butter Movie-Pop. You are busy stuffing popcorn into your face with your free hand. Oh that greasy goodness. You can practically feel your arteries closing. Yum-my.

"So I was going to put on *The Evil Dead*, but then I thought that might be a bit too close to the mark, you know?" he shrugs, and you glance out the window, where zombies are shuffling by in slow-moving packs.

"Yeah," you agree.

"So we're going with *The Lord of the Rings*," he says.

"Which ones?"

"All of them. I mean, we are gonna be here awhile, after all."

He's got a good point. If ever there is a time for a movie marathon, this is probably it.

You lose yourselves in the beautiful cinematic experience. It does get a bit uncomfortable when the orcs show up, if only because of their cognitive similarities to the horde outside the house—which, by the way, continues to grow. A few hours in, during the obligatory change-of-disc bathroom break, you hear a ruckus outside. You zip up and peer out the window in time to see one of Adam's neighbors run screaming out of his house, waiving a gun like a maniac. A zombie child is shuffling after him, and the man is screaming words even an undead kid shouldn't hear.

While you watch, the man levels the gun at the little boy's head and pulls the trigger. The boy, barely five or so, crumples to the ground. When his hand relaxes, you can see that the zombie kid has dropped something. At first you think it is a toy—a second look reveals a slender hand, wedding ring still on the third finger. It is covered in chew marks.

The man raises the gun to his own head, and you flinch away—it was bad enough to watch the last part. There's a gunshot. A moment later, to your surprise, there is angry yelling. You glance out the window again. The neighbor turned the gun on a zombie that had gotten too close, but now he is surrounded.

With horror, you watch the man look around desperately, as if to run away, but, seeing no escape, he puts the gun in his own mouth.

You don't look. The sounds are enough—the crack of a shot, then low moans and tearing, squishy sounds.

You need another drink.

"God, did you see that?!" Adam asks, aghast.

"Yeah," you say. You don't want to talk about it. "Got anything harder than beer?"

After digging around in the pantry for a few minutes, you and Adam return to your marathon, each with a tall whiskey.

Without speaking, you turn the movie on. Middle Earth was better than real Earth in some ways before; now even Middle Earth ruled by Sauron is looking pretty dandy compared to this world.

The pair of you are quite drunk by the time the movie has reached the battle for Rohan. You are literally at the edge of your seat, completely taken in by the experience, when outside you hear a loud BOOM! The room goes black.

A glance out the window confirms your theory: a zombie has managed to blow up a transformer down the block. A smell not unlike charred ham drifts toward the house.

So now not only will you not be able to finish the trilogy, you're powerless. In a zombie apocalypse. And it's getting dark. Fantastic.

"So, now what?" Adam says.

"Well," you say,

⊙ "those zombies took our finale from us. I say you and me bring the fight to them! For Rohan!" *Turn to page 114.*

⊙ "you're drunk. I'm drunk. Let's just finish the bottle of whiskey and sleep it off. Maybe when our hangovers clear, the apocalypse will be over." *Turn to page 117.*

Adam stares at you.

"Come on! We've talked about a day like this hundreds of times. In the event of a zombie apocalypse, we are gonna kick some zombie ass, remember?" You are speaking quickly, excited, leaning forward.

Adam continues his blank look. After a long pause, he says, "Are you serious? That was just drunk talk! There is pretty much no way we can actually do any of that."

"Why the hell not!?" you say. "Look, you're pretty fit, I'm nimble, we're both way smarter than those plague-ridden biddies outside." You gesture broadly. "We'll be goddamn heroes, man! We might get keys to the city and shit like that!"

"Yeah…" Adam says hesitantly. "I guess we could at least take out a few zombies, do some public good and all that."

"YES, we can," you say, perhaps a bit too exuberantly.

"But what are we going to fight with? I'm not going out there bare-handed," Adam says.

"Well," you consider. "You've got those golf clubs in the closet, that's a start. And… we could make an aerosol can into a, like, bomb! And… I dunno, what other stuff do you have around the house?"

For the next thirty minutes, you and Adam ransack his house, bringing back anything that might work as either a weapon or body armor and piling it on the couch. After a bit of sorting, you end up with: a butcher knife—as well as the rest of the knife block set—a can of air freshener with a lighter duct taped on to it, a plastic whiffle bat (Adam tossed that in. You just rolled your eyes), the metal pole from a tall lamp that Adam broke about six months ago but never threw out, a couple of putters, and, after a brief but intense debate about its usefulness as a ranged weapon, a handheld Taser.

For defense you've got a pair of shin guards, two helmets, a set of gardener's kneepads, a thick leather jacket and a considerably lighter windbreaker. When confronted about the windbreaker, Adam shrugged and said it was the best he had. And that it didn't fit him, so you'd have to wear that one.

Muttering to yourself, you accept the windbreaker—which might keep you from being bitten for a good, oh, two seconds tops—and go into the kitchen to find the lid to a large pot. You figure you can use it as both shield and battering device in close range.

You suit up. You end up with the makeshift flamethrower, a couple of knives (which you stick in your belt, but not until you've nicked yourself twice, ouch), and a heavy-weight putter. Adam, outfitted with his much-better-defensive-armor leather jacket, gets the Taser, the whiffle bat, and the long pole.

You don't speak much. You both know what must be done now. You nod to your best friend and throw open the front door.

Adam sets to with his long pole, whacking the zombie ladies back and forth. They moan and stagger back, caught off balance by this sudden threat. You dart in, slamming your putter down on the youngest zombie's head. On first impact, the putter makes a dull thud. On the second, it makes a wet "schloop" as you pull it away, and the zombie drops like a bag of rocks.

Satisfied, you step back. Adam swings in again with the pole, shoving the oldest lady off the stairs and onto the ground. Under normal circumstances, she probably would have broken a hip from the fall.

As it is, she did break a hip—you can see her whole pelvis at an odd tilt—but that doesn't stop her from getting back up again.

No time for her now—mid-life crisis woman is on you in a lurch, and you draw one of your steak knives as she gets close. Adam switches to the whiffle bat, and beats her around the head and shoulders, serving mostly as a distraction. Stupid whiffle bat. You slash at her face. She doesn't even mind when you cut her across both cheeks. She bleeds a trickling blackish fluid.

You nearly throw up. You never have been good about blood.

But Adam's there, at your back, and he shoves her away with the blunt tip of his whiffle bat before she can claw at your eyes, and you recover in time to deliver a wicked slash to her exposed throat.

In movies, that kind of thing always leads to a rather quick and simple death. Slash, done.

Not so in real life. Huh.

Even with a cut most of the way through her throat, the woman keeps attacking you. You glance at Adam. He looks as shocked as you do. You share a silent "CRAP!" in alarmed glances. But now she's at near range again, so Adam, thinking quickly, whips out the Taser and shocks her.

Zombies evidently still have an operating central nervous system. The woman instantly drops into convulsions—a pretty good sign, all things considered—and her head whips back and forth on her nearly detached neck. So gross. You pull out your biggest knife and hack at her as she spasms on the ground.

It's horrifically messy, and your pants are spattered with oozing zombie filth.

In all the gory glory, you've nearly forgotten undead granny. She grabs your ankles and tries to pull you within biting range. Adam stomps on her hands, which go flat with a crunch, but she keeps flailing. He leans down and Tasers her, too, his rubber-soled feet still stomped on her hands. She flails in an odd reenactment of a child's mummy dance. It stuns her for a few seconds, and you leap down behind her, grab her by the hair, and cut through her throat.

It still takes more than one slice, but you're improving.

The zombie falls down, permanently dead, and you stare up at Adam, panting.

You did it. You freakin' did it.

You killed some zombies.

You feel:

⊙ Elated. It was just like you imagined...but better! You're a goddamn zombie-killing hero! Those undead monsters never saw YOU coming! *Turn to page 173.*

⊙ Sick. That was the worst thing you've ever done. Those zombies are an unimaginable horror dressed as your neighbors. *Turn to page 175.*

Adam lifts one hand and opens his mouth to respond, but all that comes out is a loud belch. "Point taken," he says.

You clink your glass against his and he pours a double serving into each glass. You sit there, in the dark, drinking. Out the window you sometimes see dark shadows moving against the darkness. Periodically there are shouts or gunshots. You keep drinking.

Your bladder gives out before the bottle, and you climb the stairs to relieve yourself. You don't make it back down again; you pass a bedroom with a plush comforter that looks too inviting, and you pass out face-down. You don't stir all night.

Who knows how many hours have passed by the time you open your eyes? Your mouth feels like you ate a mattress and your eyelids are heavier than the weights you lift at the gym twice a week. When you finally pry them open, you see intense sunlight streaming in through the window.

It takes longer than usual to get to your feet through the haze of the hangover, so it is a good ten minutes before you manage to stumble back downstairs.

Later you'll blame the hangover for your oversight, but as you walk down the stairs, you don't notice the broken glass of the front window. You're rubbing your eyes blearily, standing at the bottom of the stairs, and you call out for Adam. "Hey Adam, you got any coffee? Oh, right, never mind, the power's out," you say, sleepily.

It takes you several seconds to hear the clattering noises coming from the kitchen. Maybe the power's back after all?

You go to look.

At first you think Adam was making that archetypal hangover cure, a bloody mary, but on second glance you realize that's not tomato juice smeared over the counter—that's blood.

Then Adam moans softly from behind you. You startle and turn to face your friend; his eyes are sunken and he's drooling. It's not until you see the chunk removed from his left forearm as he reaches toward you that you realize this isn't a hangover. Your best friend is a zombie now.

You:

⊙ Run like hell. *Turn to page 118.*

⊙ Put him down. You can't allow your friend to be a slavering monster for the rest of his un-life. It's the least you can do. *Turn 120.*

You high-tail it. Luckily, Adam's better physique isn't that much of an advantage when he's a zombie; he's shuffling after you, moaning quietly. Still, you're about half-hungover, your head is pounding, you aren't exactly thinking clearly, and he's moving a bit faster than you'd prefer, all things considered, since your best buddy is now trying to eat you.

Perhaps it's because you've not seen enough horror movies, or because you've seen too much disaster coverage, but either way your first instinct is to run upstairs.

You really aren't thinking all that clearly.

But anyway, you run upstairs, pulling yourself up along the handrail and leaping a few stairs at a time. When you reach the top, Adam has lumbered over to the bottom. He moans at you with chagrin, then throws himself at the stairs.

Apparently zombies aren't great stair-climbers, but by sheer brute force and repetition, he begins to climb.

Now what are you going to do? There's a zombie climbing the stairs, blocking your only escape route. Way to go, genius.

You run back into the bedroom and open the window. You lean out, considering a jump—but the streets below are full of zombies milling about. So jumping isn't looking like that great an idea.

Behind you, you hear a skidding thump; Adam probably fell down a few of the stairs. Good, you've got more time.

You have a light bulb moment, and look to the right of the window. The roof slopes, but you might be able to climb out and get to safety. You start to climb out, but fight a moment of doubt—what if you fall?

You run back in and pull the sheet off the bed. The Adam-zombie sounds like he's nearly at the top of the stairs.

You tie the twisted sheet around the leg of the bed and tug on it. Seems secure-ish? Your undead best friend is at the top of the stairs—that top step has always squeaked—and you're starting to panic. You hurriedly tie the sheet around yourself and run to the window.

You lean out, hands gripping the white molding framing the window. Are you seriously about to climb out of a window onto a sloping roof, knowing that if you slip you are going to be eaten by a horde of zombies?

You glance behind you, where zombie-Adam is standing in the doorway. His shoulders are slumped, his head leaning far to the left. His jaw is open and chewing madly.

You push yourself out of the window. For a brief second, your improvised rope is the only thing holding you up. The bed groans as it shifts across the wood floor. You lean over and clamber onto the roof.

Whew. You're safe.

You sit and try to catch your breath—your heart is pounding—when the rope around your middle tightens painfully.

Adam is yanking on the rope.

You skitter down a few inches, frantically untying the sheet before your undead friend manages to drag you off the roof or into the building. There goes your backup plan.

So, you're on the roof. You didn't really think this far ahead. It's a nice enough day, if a little cold, but at least it's not raining or anything.

You make a mental note: next time you run to safety on a roof, grab a blanket, some water, and maybe some chips. And a book or something; it's pretty boring up here.

At least you have an excellent view.

You can periodically hear your friend clattering about inside the apartment. You doze, but you can't exactly sleep well while bracing yourself against the slope. The sun is often in your eyes, and you're developing a serious tan.

It's cold at night.

After a day on the roof, you:

⊙ decide to risk re-entry. *Turn to page 122.*

⊙ stay put. Help will come eventually. *Turn to page 125.*

Friends don't let friends become horrible mindless monsters—it's one of the unwritten rules of friendship. It's so unwritten, in fact, that you never thought you'd need to uphold it.

Guess there's a time for everything.

Adam lunges for you, arms extended, and you juke backward out of the way, putting the kitchen island between you and your buddy. What you need is a weapon of some kind—luckily, you're in a kitchen, where hazards are plentiful.

The knife block is to your right; you run to it, grabbing a knife in each hand.

The zombie of your best friend moans and shuffles at you, slow, but relentless. You glance at your weapons. You've got a butcher knife—good—and…the smallest knife in the block. Well, that's inconvenient.

You throw the small knife from your non-dominant hand, awkwardly. The zombie is only a few feet away, which is lucky, because otherwise you would have completely missed. As it is, the small blade sinks into your best friend's gut. The wound seeps brackish fluid, but zombie-Adam takes no notice.

Crap.

You grab another knife from the block—this time, a steak knife, that will do—and leap backwards as the zombie of your best friend swipes at you with one hand. You return the slash with a slice from the butcher knife. The heavy blade connects with the bone of Adam's upraised forearm, and you have to pull extra-hard to get it back. The flesh from the injury is pulled back and grotesque, but Adam-zombie does not mind. It leans down, teeth bared, to bite you.

You duck and slide under his arm, stabbing again with the butcher knife, this time connecting between the ribs.

The Adam-zombie moans furiously and flails his left arm, slapping you away heavily. Even though Adam is bigger than you, most days you could bring him to an even-draw in arm wrestling. But now that he's a zombie, his limits seem to have…changed.

You stagger back from the blow, the butcher knife still sunk in Adam's rib. A blackish slow tide blossoms under Adam's crumpled and dirtied t-shirt, and now Adam-zombie leaves a trail of brown-black blood with every step.

The kitchen is a bit too small for this kind of conflict (geeze, architects should really think of these kinds of things!) and you are momentarily pinned between the fridge, the pantry, and Adam-zombie.

In a mad panicked frenzy, you scream "Aaaaaaaah!" like Tarzan and rush your zombie-friend, knife held at the level of his throat. You don't exactly have a plan, but sort of hope to either cut off his head or knock him down so you can get out.

It turns out zombies are a little bit denser than you expect, and for a brief but terrifying moment, Adam does not fall down. You hack inexpertly with the knife, striking the zombie in the neck and throat, before you push past him, but not before the zombie's claws have raked your upraised arm, leaving a bloody, ragged trail from your wrist to your elbow.

The pain hits you like a Mack truck, but you don't have a second to slow down. As soon as you are behind Adam, you reach up and cut his throat.

You will never forget that sickening moan distorted by coughs of blood. Your best friend in the world collapses to his knees, head connected to his body by the smallest strip of skin.

"I'm so sorry, Adam," you say, tears flooding your eyes. You fall to your knees and hug your friend's remains. "If only I could have saved you," you sob.

Your display of grief would probably have been fine, if it weren't for that large wound on the arm you hugged the corpse with, the one that rubbed against the bloody stab wound you gave Adam with the butcher knife, contaminating your blood stream with plague.

You have enough time to bury your friend under a pile of bricks you find in the backyard before the fever takes you. "Oh shit," you say, just before you lose consciousness.

Friends don't let friends become horrible mindless monsters—alone.

TURN TO SECTION Z
Page 181.

You think zombie-Adam has probably gone back downstairs—there was a huge clatter at about noon on the second day, so you figure it's worth it to try to get some supplies or something.

You carefully, slowly, swing yourself back into the house. You try to walk quietly; you're not exactly sure what mental capacities zombies have, but you have a feeling that if you can walk stealthily, maybe he won't sense you're there.

You look like a cartoon, trying to step quietly, feet gently, gently touching down.

The first thing you grab is the comforter off the bed. It got cold last night. Then a pillow. No, make that two.

You carefully take your haul back to the roof, tossing it at an angle onto the area next to the window. One pillow rolls down, and it's only by halfway throwing yourself out the window (one hand gripping the windowsill for dear life) that you manage to catch it and place it back higher on the roof. Your stomach hurts from where the window ledge digs in.

You turn back and tiptoe carefully, carefully into the hall. Hm. What else do you need?

There's no two ways about it: you're going to have to go downstairs. You're hungry, and you know you won't last terribly long without water. Just to be sure, you check the bathroom for some way to carry water outside, but all he has is a single glass next to the sink, which, to be honest, probably has more spit in it than you could ever safely wash out. No thanks.

You creep back to the stairs. At the last moment, your foot hovering midair, you remember the squeaky top step, and step over it with exaggerated caution.

Whew. That would have been bad.

Your heart is thudding painfully in your chest. You pause to take a few deep breaths and listen for zombie sounds.

You don't hear anything—well, nothing that's obviously inside the house. Outside there is all kinds of moaning, and shuffling, and the occasional collision with a stationary object. You shudder. That's a lot of zombies now.

Carefully, you climb down the stairs, barely daring to breathe. You don't see Adam-zombie anywhere, but that doesn't mean he's gone, though the front door is standing open, smashed clear-through. You sprint to get past the open door; hopefully none of the walkers outside saw you.

Carefully, carefully, you go to the kitchen. It's a wreck. It looks like a herd of rather belligerent drunks had a party in there.

You grab one of those eco-friendly shopping bags from the hook near the pantry and fill it. The fridge is lukewarm, and there's no bottled water, but there is beer. You take it all. The bottles clank frightfully. You pause—more moaning, but that's probably from outside.

You turn to the pantry and start shoving food in your bag, now bulging from the strain. There is a bit of fresh fruit, though the apples are rather bruised after falling on the floor. Your stomach is downright howling, and you shove one in your mouth. It's quite possibly the best food you've ever tasted.

You also grab cans of whatever; you figure the canning process probably means most of that food is good. You're about to leave with your bag when you remember to get a can opener.

Maybe it was the noise from the drawer, which was filled to bursting with metal kitchen accessories, or maybe he'd been there the whole time, but when you look up, triumphant, with the can opener in hand, you see zombie Adam, staring at you with glazed-over eyes from the doorway.

Crap.

Luckily, there are two entrances to the kitchen, so you bolt for the second one, which puts you at the other end of the living room. It must be true what they say about zombies and brains, because he follows you, even though he could probably catch you more quickly if he just turned around and went back the way he came. That means that he's only halfway in the kitchen when you sprint by with your bag of munchies.

But it's not all luck: a zombie postman in his iconic blue uniform has entered the house since you came downstairs, and he zeroes in on you. Apparently the mail isn't stopped by sleet, snow, dark of night—or death. You nearly skid into him as you try to slow down.

You throw your apple at him. It was the nearest thing you had to a weapon—it conks him right in the noggin.

No ill-effects, though maybe it bought you the half-second you needed to run up the stairs.

It's a good thing you took them at a run, too. This zombie has less of an issue with stairs, and starts to sway up and up and up toward you.

"Dammit!" you curse at him. "Couldn't the post be slow on the one day I need it to be?!"

You run back to your window, stopping on the way to flip on the stereo. Luckily it's on batteries, but you waste precious seconds tuning the thing to a station playing news, then crank the volume.

The zombie postman steps on the squeaky step. You turn the sound up higher and run for the window.

The bag is seriously weighing you down. You hoist both handles up onto your shoulder like a purse, but it's bulky and it makes it harder to climb out. You end up sidling out feet-first, clinging desperately to the sill.

The zombie mailman is lurching straight for you and you're stuck.

You wiggle your shoulders, trying to shift the bag over the edge. Crap crap crap crap he's coming closer!

You twist away, swinging out to the left of the window, just as the postman lunges toward you. He stays halfway out the window, apparently overbalanced and unable to back up, as you crawl away up the roof with your bounty.

It looks like you won't be going back inside.

It's a good thing you went back for supplies. The news reports that come in and out on the radio make things sound pretty bad out there. New York City is declared a total disaster zone. It's ten days before the Air Force begins flyovers with Black Hawk helicopters. You are sunburnt, hungry, and exhausted, but alive.

They only found a few dozen survivors in the whole city, some of them in a lot worse shape than you. They airlift you out and, after observing you in quarantine that looks an awful lot like prison "as a precautionary measure," put you on a cruise ship with thousands of other civilians. You'd think that would actually be a pretty great place to be if you're forcibly evacuated from your home, but not so. They don't even turn on the pool, you're given a room with a stranger who you rarely see but who smells like feces, and the shows are just terrible, true abominations of theatre.

At least no one here is trying to eat you, though. Yet.

The military is going in. The entire Eastern Seaboard has been evacuated. The United States of America is now at war—with its undead self.

YOU SURVIVE. CONGRATULATIONS.

THE END

Heck no, you're not going back there! Your best buddy, the guy who was there when you got fired from your job and made sure you got thoroughly trashed at a bar to forget about it, who is always up for a meal at that disgusting pizza joint that no one else will go to because it looks so foul but is really so good, who has known you since college and still likes you regardless, has become a horrible monster and you'll probably never forgive yourself. But you also don't want to go back in there and face him, because there's a chance he'll kill you or turn you into a horrible monster, too.

He never did like to do things alone.

So you sit there, on the roof, hugging your knees. The roof gets hot during the day and cold at night. You haven't eaten anything you'd call a 'meal' in about a day, even before you got on the roof—all that beer didn't help. And you know what turns out to not be so good for a hangover? Hanging out in the sun on the roof while a horde of zombies mills around below you.

It's also incredibly boring. You try to doze, your knees pulled up to your chest and braced against the slope of the roof, but your rest is fitful, at best.

Down below, the group of zombies grows. You're sickened as you see children, some as young as four or five, shuffling along with the bigger adult zombies. From the looks of it, the plague wasn't picky; people of all ages, races, and professions are moaning by.

A house down the street catches on fire, and the building burns for hours. No one comes to subdue the flames. You start to wonder if it will eventually burn to Adam's house—the homes here aren't too far apart. You walk the perimeter of the roof, thinking maybe there is a way you can jump from this building to the next, but every time you try to jump your knees quake and you lose your nerve. You settle back down and watch the flames burn closer. Maybe the fire won't be able to make the jump, either.

As the days pass, you keep thinking someone—the Army, or the Red Cross, or a rogue zeppelin, anyone—is going to come help you and the other people of New York, so you stay there, waiting.

No one comes. Blame exposure, dehydration, or the beginnings of starvation; it doesn't matter which, so take your pick. You're dead, sprawled on the roof under the unyielding sun.

THE END

"Yeah," Adam says, rubbing his face blearily with one hand. "Yeah, that's a good idea." He yawns just like a lion, with a trumpeting undertone. "Yeah, let's just grab some of the blankets and go to sleep down here."

You fill your arms with an overstuffed down blanket and shlep it into the living room—only to find Adam had seen you headed that way and made a dash for the couch. He's already stretching out there as you lumber over. "Hey! I wanted the couch!" you protest.

"Tough cookies," Adam says. "I'm taller, anyway, I should get the couch." And he rolls over, not even willing to do you the courtesy of fighting. Man, not fair.

You take your bundle of blanket and huff over to the La-Z-Boy. It may be part of the house defenses now, but you had the foresight to position it with the back against the bookcase, so it's still serviceable as a makeshift bed. You flop down into it, recline enough to put your feet up, and snuggle under the blanket.

You wake up to the sound of breaking glass in the next room. You wipe the drool off your face and clamber out of the chair, which is refusing to fold up.

As you finally round the corner to peer into the living room, you see with great horror that even the NBA is not immune to the zombie plague. Those windows you and Adam didn't bother to board up because they were too tall for anyone to reach?

Not true if the zombie in question is seven feet tall.

You don't watch enough sports to know which one of the Knicks is trying to break in the window to eat you, but you have a feeling a giant athletic zombie that can't feel pain is a considerably bigger (no pun intended) threat than your average zombie.

You stare in open-mouthed horror until Adam comes careening around the corner from the kitchen.

"Don't just stand there, idiot, he'll be in any moment now!" he screams at you. "Grab some of the supplies and come upstairs with me."

Awoken from your reverie, you run full-tilt to the kitchen and start piling up supplies on one of the blanket, creating a massive Santa's sack full of survival necessities. You're hefting it up onto your back when Adam comes running back.

"Good, great, I'll get the water," he says, the words a blur.

You don't have air left to breathe; this pack is really heavy. You bend over nearly double as you schlep the bundle up the stairs.

There's a crash of breaking wood as you reach the top and sag the bag to the ground. Adam comes running up the stairs behind you.

"Move move! I've got as much of the water as I could carry," he says.

"We can't stay here at the top of the stairs."

"Why not?" you ask, your breath coming in heavy wheezes. "This seems fine." You sag down to rest on your knees.

"Get your lazy ass up," Adam barks. "Look, I figure our safest place is the crawl space in the attic. We can haul our stuff in there and block the door. There's only one way in there."

And, you think to yourself, only one way out.

There's another crash, and a moan that sounds like it might be coming from the living room.

"Maybe, maybe they can't climb stairs?" you say.

"Moron, we already know they can. My front door is up four steps from the street and we've had old lady zombie pounding on it for a day now," Adam says, gathering up half of the supplies from your pouch to make one of his own.

"Oh," you say. You can't help it. You don't think well when you first wake up.

"Come on!" Adam says, shoving you with his leg as he walks by. "We'll be safer up there."

Begrudgingly, you pull together your survival sack and follow Adam up the narrow stairway, then up the thin wooden step ladder he pulls from the ceiling of one bedroom. It takes some wrangling, but you manage to haul your load up there, and Adam shoves it into a corner. You both return to the pile for more, and together carry almost everything up. On your last trip, you see that the undead basketball star has smashed into the furniture several times, and the La-Z-Boy is no longer holding the front door closed. The bookshelf begins to sway. The superstar zombie moans at you and shuffles—if you can call it that when a monster has a seven-foot stride—toward the stairs.

The attic suddenly seems like a great idea.

Adam doesn't let you go up yet, though. "We need to slow them down," he says.

"What?! I just want to get in that attic already!" you protest. You really hate this whole end-of-the-world thing. You're starting to crack a little around the edges.

"No, I'm serious. We've got to push some of the furniture into the stairway so they can't climb up as easily." Adam can be really insistent.

With a groan, you follow Adam back to one of the bedrooms. While he busily unscrews the bed so you can shove it in the stairway, you wrestle the mattress up the ladder—hey, if you're going to be stuck in the attic, you might as well make it more comfortable up there.

In a moment of clarity, you take a hammer to the ceiling in the bathroom.

"What the hell are you doing?!" Adam screams when he hears your clamor.

"I," you say snidely, "am giving us a way to access the bathroom while we are trapped in the attic. "Or did you plan on us staying in the attic for that, too?"

Adam's jaw opens and then closes again. Finally he comes out with, "Do you have any idea how much it cost me to get those tiles?!"

"You won't have any need for them at all if we don't survive this!" you say, and return to smashing a hole in the ceiling.

Half an hour later, Adam has more or less filled the stairway with various furniture, and you have made a person-sized hole in the ceiling of the bathroom, if you squeeze a bit. You also barricade the bathroom door with a chair you brought in behind you. You climb out through the attic-floor hole, leaving the bathroom locked and barricaded from the inside.

"You'll thank me later," you say to Adam when he stares at the foot-and-a-half wide hole.

The zombies below have smashed through your preliminary defenses and are moaning about. You count at least six down there. You're suddenly glad for Adam's "barricade-the-stairs" idea.

It's now early-afternoon and you are both ravenous, so you both retreat up to the attic, pulling the folding ladder up behind you.

The attic is what you might call half-finished. There's only the barest bit of insulation, but nails only poke through in the corners, where it's really too far for you to crawl anyway. The floor is plain plywood, except where you've put the mattress, and your ragged hole to the bathroom fits nicely along the middle of the wall.

You have a meal of canned soup, eaten cold from the can, washed down with water from one of your jugs. Adam unscrews a metal vent cover, so you have a six-inch window to the outside. The roof isn't quite tall enough for either of you to stand fully straight, so you mostly half-crouch to walk around. There are two boxes of Christmas and Halloween decorations Adam didn't clear out sitting in a corner.

You are up there for a long time. You're not entirely sure how many days you pass up there. Cabin fever sets in by day two. There's just nothing to do up there. Adam is eventually grateful for the bathroom access, though he might not ever forgive the smash job you used for it. You have flushable water for awhile, so it only begins to smell after a week or so. You feel serious sympathy for Anne Frank. The boredom is so intense Adam lowers the ladder once and you both go running for entertainment items: a deck of cards, a board game, an armful of books. Adam nearly got eaten by a zombie trying to decide on which board game to bring up, and you had to scramble to get back to safety.

You don't go down again, but at least now you can play Solitaire or Monopoly. Finally, you have more than enough time to play a whole game of Monopoly.

You have a tendency to snack when you're bored, but Adam puts an end to that after he realizes you've gone through a whole bag of chips by yourself in one afternoon. After that, he "rations" the food, which means he guards it all on his side of the attic. Even so, your food runs out more quickly than you would have expected.

One night, just before you light your last candle and are sitting down to have the Very Important "what's the next step" talk, you hear a whistling sound overhead. You and Adam pause and both try to look out of the little vent-hole. There's a CRASH, and an explosion in the distance. It's the first of many.

Someone—maybe Korea, or Canada, China, Russia, or…maybe even U.S. military—has begun a bombing campaign of New York City.

"Holy shit!" you say. "They're going to blow us all up!"

"What the hell do we do now?" Adam asks, his voice borderline hysterical.

You respond, "We…

⊙ "duck and cover and pray like hell?" *Turn to page 131.*

⊙ "make a run for it!" *Turn to page 132.*

You drag yourself up the stairs, yawning just about every third step. You haven't worked this hard or been this tired in ages.

You barely take time to unmake the bed before you slide into the sheets and curl up to sleep.

You must have had a really good dream, because you wake yourself up with the moaning.

Wait…no you don't. That wasn't you moaning. There's someone in the room with you.

You sit bolt upright. In the early morning light you can see two shapes moving in the bedroom.

Suddenly you hear Adam calling your name. He runs around the corner and stops, wide-eyed with fear.

"I just woke up," he says, stumbling over the words. "I was going to get a bottle of water when I saw the window was broken. I…I…."

A zombie plops onto the bed next to you, and you scream and pull away, smacking at it with one hand.

You try to clamber out of bed, but the sheets are too tight and your leg gets tangled.

Adam is crying in the doorway, paralyzed by fear.

You scream to him for help, but he doesn't move, doesn't stir, just sobs into his hands as a zombie you can't even see bites you hard on the neck. In the second before your eyes close, you see more zombies encircling Adam. You can hear his screams even as you fall into blackness.

TURN TO SECTION Z
Page 181.

"I mean," you continue. "Outside we've got who knows how many zombies. The missiles could miss us. We're probably better off in here until they stop, then we can get out and run for it and there will be a lot fewer zombies for us to deal with."

Adam reluctantly agrees. You blow out the candle and take turns standing at the vent, listening to the roar of military aircraft and the scream of missiles. America has never seen an attack of this kind on her soil before. It is horrible to watch. You can't turn away.

Adam starts crying when the skyscrapers catch fire. You can't blame him. It is just too much to watch. Too much to think about.

The planes come closer, and you and Adam hug each other, crying terrified tears and muttering half-remembered prayers. "Now I lay me down to sleep, oh please oh please oh please God don't let me be killed by missiles…"

Your feeble prayers are no match for the might of air-to-ground weaponry. Adam's beautiful mid-19th century brownstone is shaken apart. It didn't take a direct strike for the masonwork to crumble. The house collapses under you. If anyone were to look for your remains, they would have to dig through several tons of rubble to find it.

But no one looks. New York City is wiped from the map.

THE END

The drone of the planes gets louder as you devise your plan: get downstairs, run away from any zombies, find a car and drive like hell.

It's simple, but there's the beauty of it.

You slide through the hole to the bathroom, hefting the metal chair out of the way and shoving it, feet first, into the hallway in front of you. Adam comes behind, carrying the hammer ominously. It takes you a few minutes to realize the second floor is empty. At least, you aren't under immediate attack. It's clear that the undead did get up here; the blockade furniture has been shoved aside or off the edge of the staircase and the bannister is splintered and broken.

"Okay, let's go," you call to Adam. You are suddenly aware of how hungry you've been the past few days, but there isn't exactly enough time to have a snack.

The light of an explosion illuminates the windows in the bedroom. "Let's move!" Adam shouts, and shoves furniture back down the stairs. You trade your chair-weapon for a golf club and follow your friend down.

A swing to the head with the putter puts down the first zombie you see, and you and Adam outrun the rest in the house, leaping out the front window. You land awkwardly, and your ankle twinges, but this isn't a time to go sit on the bench. There are a lot of zombies out here.

"Aaaah!" Adam screams as he fights off a group of preteen girl zombies. They look like they got infected in the middle of a Taylor Swift concert; they're all rhinestones and pink ribbons. One has a "I LOVE YOU TAYLOR" shirt.

You take extra pleasure in beating them with your club.

"Adam, where is a car?" you scream over the hum of the planes overhead and the moans of the zombies around you.

"This way!" he says, darting to the side after slashing the claw end of the hammer at another zombie.

You run down the road, juking the slow-moving zombies if you can, smacking them with the golf club if you can't. You have to run half a block before you see a taxi, the driver slumped forward over the wheel.

"That's it, let's go!" you scream. That last explosion was a little too close for comfort.

You run to the car and pull open the door. There is only half the driver left. Your throat fills with bile as you pull the man out of the seat to crumple in the road.

You take the wheel and lean over to let Adam in. He's in close combat with an undead Middle Eastern man, and it takes him several seconds before he can get in. Your screaming "GET IN NOW" at him probably didn't help, but you like to feel like he maybe needed the extra encouragement.

You haven't driven in years—you live in New York, after all—but you remember the basics and slam your foot on the gas. Zombies thump thump THUMP across your hood and under your wheels, but you don't slow down.

The good thing about an apocalypse might be the lack of city traffic. Lots of abandoned cars to drive around, sure, but no one in them to worry about pissing off.

You drive like a maniac, not even sure quite where you're going. Eventually, Adam nods off.

Except when he wakes up, something is different. He's holding his head loosely on his shoulders and staring at you. He moans.

Holy shit you are trapped in a car with a zombie of your best friend!

The good news is Adam remembered his seat belt, so the zombie is moderately restrained. But it's not easy to drive with a zombie slapping at you with his clawed hands or snapping his teeth together a mere inches from your face.

You would probably be forgiven for your bad driving, accordingly. But...brick walls aren't very forgiving. You're so busy fighting off the zombie that you don't look where you're driving, and slam directly into a building.

Luckily, it's the head-on collision that kills you both instantly, so you don't have to deal with the ethics of killing a zombified best friend.

THE END

You continue working as usual, except... except you're feeling really good now. Your head doesn't hurt anymore, but the floors are sort of wobbling under your feet and it's really hard to walk straight and you've started hiccuping.

As you walk through the workroom your gaze falls on the copy machine. Heh. You've always wanted to play with the copy machine. Hey, why the hell not?!

You open the machine, tossing the stack of papers on top into the trash with drunken abandon, and smoosh your face on the glass. You push the big green button—you love that big green button!—and forget to close your eyes in time. You stand up, blinking, as the machine whirrs and grinds, and a few seconds later your face, your hilarious face, shows up in the out tray. Awesome!

After three or four times, photocopying your face doesn't seem fun anymore, but then you have, like, the best idea ever. You unbutton your pants and heft yourself up onto the copy machine, giggling like a maniac.

The machine makes 12 beautiful copies of your butt before your giggling starts to draw attention. A murmuring crowd gathers at the doorway. Then Lisette shows up.

"HEY boss!" you slur. "Ya wanna play with the copier, too? I betcha your ass would make some great" hiccup "copies."

"Get. Down. From. There. This. Instant!" Lisette says, pulling on your arm. "And put your pants back on!"

You slide off the copier clumsily and fumble with your zipper, only getting it halfway secured before you give up. "Hey," you say. "Hey Lisette, want me to autogra- authografft—want me to sign one for ya?"

You grab a copy of your tuchus and a marker and sign your name in exaggerated loopy letters, then you shove the page at your boss. "You can frame it if ya want," you say, gravely.

"What is wrong with you?" Lisette demands. She doesn't even accept your fine artwork.

"I—" you start, then struggle and start over again. "I was shick. But then I took shom medichin, and now I'm grrrreat. Great, I tell you." You purse your lips and consider for a moment. "Listhet? I think you probly need some medichin too. Might make you nicther."

Lisette's face turns a peculiar shade of burgundy. "Out! Out! You are FIRED, you hear me, FIRED!"

She starts shoving you toward the elevator. She's screaming: "You go and don't come back tomorrow. And I will tell everyone I know how reprehensible a person you are, and you will be blacklisted in the industry. Good luck ever finding a job again!" she yells as she throws you against the back of the elevator. She leans in, pushes the button for the ground floor, and ducks out before the doors close.

When the elevator arrives at the bottom, two angry-looking men in dark jackets are waiting for you. "Hey fellas," you say cordially. "There's a really angry lady upstairs, you should probly check on her."

They don't acknowledge your advice. They pick you up by the elbows and drag you out the front door of the building, letting you collapse in a heap on the pavement.

They stand ominously at the entrances. You make faces at them as you brush the dirt off your clothes and stand up.

You start walking. At least it's a nice day.

You:

⊙ head toward home. *Turn to page 82.*

⊙ wander to Central Park. The walk will give you time to sober up. *Turn to page 136.*

The park isn't that far away, and it's a lovely day, so why not enjoy a nice walk?

You're walking along, minding your own business, when you hear moaning. At first you disregard it—probably just another schulb trying to get over a crappy day at the office—but then it keeps happening, loud enough that you can clearly hear it.

You stop and look around.

That's when you notice: everyone on the street looks…odd. They're holding their heads at a slump, have a vacant expression, and seem to be having trouble walking. A woman missing a shoe comes closer, and she has what looks like blood on her shirt.

So does the man there, with the ripped jeans.

And they're coming toward you.

You start walking again, a little faster. Maybe you can just get away from them.

You round a corner—the others are moving slowly, at least, and it was easy enough to get out of sight—and…there are more people, sort of milling about in the street.

This… this may not have been your best idea.

They kinda…well, this is hard to swallow, but all those people kinda look like zombies.

You do a double-take, glancing at the postal worker shuffling toward you from the left. His blue uniform is torn at the shoulder, and blood is covering his face. Yeah…he definitely looks like a zombie.

You panic and run up the street, ducking into an alley. This won't be a good hiding place for long.

Your gaze falls upon the trash bin a little deeper in the alley. It reeks to high heaven.

That's it! In about every zombie movie, the undead can be fooled if you don't smell good and kinda shuffle like they do! Perfect!

Rumpling your clothing as you head for the dumpster—untucked shirt, hair disheveled, one shoe untied—you hesitate only for a second before climbing up and throwing yourself on the heap of rotting garbage.

There must be an Italian place nearby, because there is half-eaten spaghetti sauce everywhere. The smell is so intense you vomit, the remainder of your lunch adding to your tres chic dumpster look. You smear yourself with sauce and filth.

Thoroughly sullied, you climb back out of the dumpster and head for the street, dragging one foot behind you in a lame impression of Quasimodo. This had better work, or not only are you probably going to die but you'll also have willingly jumped into garbage for no good reason.

Moment of truth. You moan softly and shuffle out of the alleyway. A few of the undead shuffle toward you, but you moan and shift slightly out of the way. They don't seem to notice. Maybe they think the sauce is blood? Oh, right, they don't think at all, but it doesn't matter much because you're alive.

You keep walking, hoping you'll find someone who can help you. It's hard to look around while you're pretending to be a zombie. Luckily, you're not far from the park, and you soon hear the clop-clop-clop of a mounted police officer.

"Thank goodness," you say quietly, slowly shuffling toward the horse. "Please, you have to help me get out of here. They're real zombies. I'm pretending to be a zombie, and they haven't noticed yet but they might at any moment..."

You look up at the officer you're supplicating.

But that's not an officer. At least, not anymore. And it's not a horse, either. There's a gash in the horse's flank as big as your palm.

You'll never know for sure if it was the talking or the smell of spaghetti that gave you away, because you are murdered...crushed under the hooves of a pale undead horse.

THE END

So here it is, probably the end of the world, and you're stuck at home by yourself. Figures.

You think about calling your ex, but no, now you'll seem even more desperate than the last time you talked. You sigh and peer out the blinds of your window.

Down below, it looks pretty mundane and serene. The traffic isn't moving, but you can pretend it's a bad traffic jam. People are milling around in the street. If you don't think about it much, you can pretend they aren't cannibalistic undead monsters—they're just regular folks, going about their days. And really, deep down, aren't we all monsters in our own way?

Damn it, you always get melancholy when you're alone too much.

You sit down at your computer and surf the web for a while, but your home screen is covered with sensationalized stories headlined "NEW YORK IN CRISIS," "SLEEPLESS CITY FACES MONSTER THREAT" and "DEAD STREETWALKERS IN NYC" (sounds like that editor got rather confused). The images are graphic and one of the ads is the really annoying kind that automatically plays a video every time it loads, so you put away your laptop and grab a book.

That's fine for a while, but eventually your back starts to cramp. There's just no comfortable way to sit: you try laying on your back, holding the book in the air, but your arms get tired; you roll on your belly, but your neck starts to ache; you sit up, but by now you've developed a crick, so you give up on that, too.

You wander your apartment, looking for something to do. This really sucks.

You take out the cat puzzle your grandma gave you for Christmas a couple of years ago. Under the image of the tabby cat sleeping among a pile of adorable antiques, the box says "5000 pieces!" It's pretty enthusiastic about being so complicated. You clear a space on the dining room table and start looking for the corners and edge pieces.

You work on that puzzle for three days. You only stop to eat, pee, or sleep, and you're considerably bored, so you do a lot of those things.

When you finally put the last goddamn piece in the puzzle, you don't feel accomplished. You feel defeated. You hate yourself more than a little bit for having wasted so much of your life on that stupid sleeping cat.

In a fit of cabin-fever-induced rage, you shove all the puzzle pieces to the floor and storm out of your apartment.

Outside, the air is clear and crisp. The sky is blue, and you can hear birds singing. You take in a long deep breath—

—And are attacked by the quartet of zombies you passed on your way out.

Ah well. At least Grandma will be happy to know you finally finished that puzzle.

TURN TO SECTION Z
Page 181.

There is general consensus that a zombie tied to a rolling chair isn't really much of a threat, so everyone figures Alyssa is safe enough. Besides, people are fairly well accustomed to avoiding her anyway, so now they just have an extra incentive.

"And there's the benefit of making it look like she's still working, in case Lisette comes by to check on us," Becky says. You think she's joking. Maybe.

You:

⊙ Say, "We need to plan our next move, people." *Turn to page 31.*

⊙ Decide to leave. You've officially had enough of this place. *Turn to page 82.*

⊙ Suggest everyone play a rousing game of Roll the Zombie. *Turn to page 146.*

Because you're not really sure the strength or infection capacity of your average zombie, you agree that the safest thing to do is secure her.

After a brief discussion, you decide the best zombie-storage area in the near vicinity is the boss's office. Lisette isn't anywhere around, so you don't even have to ask permission—even better!

You wheel the teeth-grinding Alyssa-zombie over to the office and push her in. Bruce thinks she should stay tied up; Becky pretty much thinks it doesn't matter. You leave her tied to her rolling chair, turn off the lights, and close the door. There's another debate over whether or not zombies can open doors. You give up on the argument when Bruce brings up the raptors in Jurassic Park.

"Okay, fine, we'll secure the door. Bruce, since this is your fault, help me carry the couch in from the waiting room," you say.

He obliges, and the two of you haul the battered fake-leather couch in, shoving it against the office door—which opens inward. You figure it's good enough.

The three of you leave, congratulating yourselves on resolving an odd problem, only to have Lisette storm into the workroom 15 minutes later.

"What. The. Hell. Have you done. To. My. Office," she barks.

"We barricaded it," Bruce says. "You'll thank us later."

"Th-…Thank you? What is wrong with you people?" Lisette is practically spewing hatred right now.

You're almost enjoying this.

"Lisette, it's not a big deal. You weren't around for us to ask, but your office was the best place to keep her," you say in a conciliatory voice that doesn't at all match your inner glee.

"Keep her? Keep WHO?!" Lisette has always had a penchant for yelling when she doesn't understand something.

"Alyssa," Becky says simply. "She turned into a zombie so we had to lock her in your office to protect the safety of everyone else."

Lisette's cheeks burn red and her eyes flash, but she says nothing. She turns and walks back to her office. With a look at the others, you follow her. You find her pushing on the heavy couch, trying to dislodge it from the door.

"You don't want to do that," you tell her.

"Help me move this couch immediately. The office is not the place for this kind of behavior," Lisette says.

"Lisette, I'm sorry you're mad, but look, I can't let you go in there," you say, maintaining your calm. It's a struggle to keep from rolling your eyes.

"I believe I am the authority figure here and I will make those kind of de—" she breaks off, staring into the window to her office. "What's that?"

she says, alarmed.

"It's Alyssa. Becky wasn't kidding when she said she'd been turned into a zombie," you say. "Look, we don't know much about what's going on, but we felt it best that we lock her up."

"Omigod," she says, the color draining out of her face. "Zom-zombies? Like, real ones? Those movies used to give me the worst nightmares."

You've never seen Lisette look so frightened, not even when management said they would be "letting people go."

"I've got this well in hand," you say, feeling a twinge—just a twinge, of course—of empathy for the botoxed bitch. "You don't need to worry about it, okay Lisette?"

Lisette looks at you with blank fear in her eyes. She nods quietly.

Huh. Figures it took a zombie uprising for you to get a leadership role in this place.

⊙ *Turn to page 33.*

Y ou pick up the phone in Alyssa's cubicle and dial the three digits. A three-chime bell rings in your ears painfully.

Oh yeah, you forgot to dial out. These stupid phones and this stingy corporation. Won't even let you do the basics without Big Brothering you.

You dial again, remembering to first dial one before your number.

The phone rings, and you turn back to face the gathered crowd. Alyssa-the-zombie is trying to bite her own shoulder, causing the chair to spin counter-clockwise. You idly smack her on the head, and she looks up as if startled.

"Hellowhat'syouremergency," a female voice on the other end of the line says. She's frantic.

"Um, well, one of my coworkers has gotten sick or rabid or crazy or something," you say. How do you explain this?

"Hehehehehehe," the voice chitters. The laugh has no trace of pleasure or humor in it. It sounds a little insane. There's no other answer.

"Hello?" you say.

The tittering laugh comes back. "Heeheheh, I have no idea what to tell you. This whole city is going crazy, crazy! If your friend there has the plague, the best thing you can do is push them off the building. But then," the voice pauses, "it may already be too late for you. God have mercy. You're probably gonna die soon."

The operator hangs up.

Stunned, you slowly put the phone back on the cradle.

"Huh," is all you say. You report back the conversation. "And then she hung up on me," you finish.

Several of the coworkers listening go a bit pale.

"I have no idea what we should do," you say. You pull the wheeled chair restraining the zombie Alyssa back toward you; she'd started scooting out of the cubicle, toward Nick and his mustard-covered tie. Maybe zombies have a thing for mustard?

After a pregnant pause, you say, "Do we...

◉ leave her here? She's pretty well tied up." *Turn to page 140.*

◉ lock her in an office and hope for the best?" *Turn to page 141.*

◉ kill her?" *Turn to page 144.*

B ruce and Becky look grim, but each nod in turn.

"It does seem like the only thing we can really do now," Becky says.

"Really, it's kind of the merciful thing," Bruce agrees, speaking slowly.

The group pauses, contemplating.

"So how are we going to do it?" you say, eventually.

This is a conundrum. You all were aware of the general zombie lore, but who knows if it's real or effective against this kind of zombie outbreak? What if you kill her only to have her get back up again?

And besides, this is your friend—yes, now you'll admit it, she was your friend, not just your coworker—you're killing.

You've never killed so much as a cockroach—you always have to call the super when one is scuttling in your kitchen.

"We could push her off the roof, like the 9-1-1 operator suggested," Becky says. "Even if it didn't work, she wouldn't be our problem anymore."

You all consider this a moment. "Okay. Do we have other options?" you ask.

"Electrocution?" Bruce ventures. "Poison her with chemicals? We could always hit her with something really hard in the head. That seems effective in the movies."

"Yeah," you say. You pause for a moment. "I don't think I could hit her," you admit. "Or get her to drink any bleach or whatever."

"And shocking someone intentionally seems hard to control," Becky agrees.

"Could we crush her under the freight elevator or something?" Bruce suggests.

"How would we get her underneath it?" you ask. "No, I think we have to go with the easiest answer: Let's push her out a window."

The other two agree. There are only a handful of windows on the floor that open, but you only need one. You push Alyssa-zombie into an executive office—passing right by your boss and not bothering to explain what's going on—and open a window.

"We'll have to lift her up to get her over," you say.

"Should we untie her first?" Bruce asks.

"No, what if she breaks free? Then what would we do?" Becky says.

"Right. So we throw her, chair and all, out the window? Okay. Let's lift her up," you say.

It takes all three of you to hoist the chair over the ledge. Zombie Alyssa isn't helping things; she keeps trying to bite the cords tying her wrist. She doesn't seem to mind if she bites her wrist in the process. It's grotesque.

"Alyssa, I'm sorry about this. I hope you'd understand," you say. You are trying to have a moment here, but Alyssa isn't cooperating. Her own brackish blood is dribbling down her chin.

"Yeah," Bruce says.

"Let's get this done," Becky says, and shoves hard.

The rolling chair with a zombie office worker attached flies out the window. You and the others lean out and watch as the chair tilts and tumbles to land face-down on the pavement with a THUNK. The wheels spin for several seconds.

You feel a bit sick.

Bruce says, "Come on, let's get this figured out." You follow numbly.

⊙ *Turn to page 32.*

"We could roll her back and forth down the hallway! She's not gonna complain, and it would be a lot of fun!" you say. The more you talk about it, the more this idea grows on you.

"You are a moron," Becky says, and walks away.

Bruce shakes his head and leaves.

"Come on, nobody thinks that would be fun?" you say, a slight whine in your voice.

"I guess I'd play," Johnny says.

"Excellent!" you say, and start to roll Alyssa-zombie into the hallway. "If anyone else wants to play with us, come out in the hall."

You stand at one end and Johnny stands at the other side of the long hallway, Alyssa-zombie between you, thrashing in her chair. You decide the game is like capture-the-flag, but with a zombie. At the count of three, you both run as fast as you can for Alyssa-zombie. The first person to grab her chair and pull her back, wins.

"Okay, okay, ready?" you call, laughing between each word.

"Sure, whatever," Johnny says. What a hipster. He's totally into it, too.

"One…two….three!" You run for the center. Alyssa is biting at the air, moaning in what sounds like a snarl. Johnny gets there first and grabs the back of the chair, surprising you by pushing the zombie toward you at first. Clever kid, he's using her as a zombie weapon.

"Hey, watch it," you say, when the zombie's teeth get close.

Johnny just laughs and runs back to his side, pulling the chair with one hand. Alyssa turns and bites at his fingers at the top of the chair.

"Okay, you win that round," you say, laughing. "Put'er back, we'll go again."

Johnny sullenly slumps back to the middle with his zombie prize and returns to his side.

"One…twothree," you say, cheating and running out faster this time. Alyssa is facing you, and you don't bother with spinning the chair—you run backward toward your side of the hall. Johnny isn't having that, and pulls on the chair from the other direction.

You're mid-contest—Alyssa in the middle thrashing to bite someone, anyone—when you hear someone shrilly say, "This is no way to behave in a professional environment!"

Both you and Johnny freeze and look up to find the source of the voice. It's Matthew, your boss's personal assistant. He's a total brown-nosing fun-ruining prick.

"Go away, Matthew," you sneer. "We're busy with a bit of 'group bonding.'" You can't keep the singsong from your voice.

"This is abhorrent! Playing games in the office?!" Matthew says, snippy as always. "I can have you written up for this."

"Fine, Matthew!" you say, turning to face him. "Fine, go right ahead. It's not like it's going to matter, because this place isn't going to be here much longer. If you didn't notice, people are turning into zombies."

You gesture down at Alyssa for emphasis. Bad timing; the zombie had lunged forward and her teeth clip your hand, drawing blood.

"Dammit! Look what you've done, Matthew!" you hold your bleeding hand up. "Dammit!"

Johnny has by now slunk away. Predictable.

Matthew points his nose into the air. "Serves you right," he says, and wheels on his heel to go back into the office.

Muttering to yourself, you wheel Alyssa-zombie back into the cube farm and sit glumly at your desk. The bite isn't all that severe, but it starts to throb in earnest after a few minutes. You go to the bathroom to rinse it out. You're still there when the chest pains start.

You realize, as you sink to the floor clutching your chest, that there's a lesson in this experience. Perhaps 'Zombies are not toys'? No, that's not quite right.

Oh yes, you've got it. 'Matthew is a dick and it's all his fault.'

The only good news is you might infect him along the way, too.

TURN TO SECTION Z
Page 181.

Your only survival-type training was a camp-out in your backyard when you were ten (and your mom made you come inside after it got dark because she thought it looked like rain, so your camping adventure was mostly watching movies and eating microwaved s'mores) and a few months where you were deeply interested in survivalist TV shows, but the overall effect of those was making you sure you never ever ever wanted to be stranded on Everest in a snowstorm or anywhere where you might be required to drink your own pee.

So letting Bruce take the reins seems like the best possible idea.

"Um, hey Bruce, could you go over your plan again? I want to be sure I really get it," you say, trying to make up for the fact that you were completely ignoring his speech the first time.

"Right," Bruce says, his shoulders already squared away in the best mock-military stance since Patton. "First, we secure our floor from incursion from below. Then, we go floor by floor, speaking with the other offices. Anyone who likes our plan can join us. Anyone who doesn't will be forced to move to an unsecured floor lower down—we don't want to risk unsavory sorts being in our midst, do we? No, we don't." He didn't even pause to let anyone else chime in. You get a little shiver of anxiety.

"We are to prepare for eminent attack. We will arm ourselves with whatever we can find or make. We consolidate supplies, prepare defenses, and ready the building as best we can." Bruce leans forward on the table, his arms seeming all muscle. "And then," he says, looking quietly around the room with a slow gaze, "we survive."

Gulp.

Steve is visibly shaking, but Becky steps forward and confidently asks, "Where do we start?"

Bruce gives her a smile that could cut diamonds. "There are three points of ingress to this floor: a stairwell on either side of the floor and the elevator. We blockade the stairways first, on the downward side. The elevator is working now but we might lose power at any moment, so we block that area, too. We'll need to make part of the defenses portable so we can move to the other floors, but defense is the priority. Let's gather up everyone on the floor, and divide into teams to PROTECT. OUR. BUILDING!"

You meet Bruce's roar with a weak "yeah!"

Everyone stares at you, and you shift on your feet awkwardly. "Okay then," you say.

Bruce designates himself as the leader overall. You're put in charge of the east stairwell with Becky; Kristina, Alex, and Steve are to work on the west one; and Bruce goes off to find people to boss around for the elevator protection.

The next few hours are a surreal nightmare—spending all day doing manual labor with your officemates? No thank you. Together you break down cubicle barriers and tables, forming a mishmash barricade down in the stairwells and across the elevator doors. You are hot and tired and you hate your coworkers more than you ever thought possible—you thought filling out a form with these people was bad; well, it's nothing compared to negotiating a working barricade.

You slink back into the workroom and rest your head on your crossed arms on the table. After you-don't-know-how-long, more of your coworkers, including Our Great Leader Bruce, trickle in.

"Okay," Bruce says, confident in his own plans. "Now we need to start working with the other floors. I'll stay here and organize the supply chain. Becky, will you be our ambassador to the lower floors?" Bruce says. Great, now he has a favorite student. Becky, ever the organized mind, nods her assent. "And I need someone else to take the upper floors. Any volunteers?"

You:

⊙ Check on Alyssa. Why hasn't she been helping?! *Turn to page 29.*

⊙ Your stomach is rumbling. It's probably time everyone had something to eat. You propose a break for dinner. *Turn to page 35.*

⊙ You've had enough of being bossed around. You're going home. Bruce can suck it. You get up and leave. *Turn to page 82.*

⊙ Volunteer to check upstairs. *Turn to page 160.*

Without bothering to think too much about the situation, you plunge into the smoke after Steve. "GODDAMMIT STEVE," you yell, coughing heavily. "Get back here!"

Steve has run toward what is possibly the darkest, scariest corner of the building.

"Damn you, Steve, you are such a jerk and I am going to beat the shit out of you after I catch you," you say, panting now in the heat. Flames are climbing up the wall next to you, devouring a mock-impressionist painting that has always looked like a ball of tangled twine to you. Good riddance.

You can't see Steve anywhere, but up ahead, you hear a cry.

"Steve, I'm coming!" you call, bursting into another fit of coughing. You run toward the sound.

Steve has literally run himself into a corner. He must have been trying to open a door, thinking it might be a way out (it's actually a janitor's closet), but a skittering of fire closed after him and now he's backed into the corner.

He panics when he sees you and goes running again, back in the direction of the front of the building. But he didn't even bother to jump, and he doesn't get two steps before the flames are climbing his leg. Feeling the heat, Steve screams, a sickening cry of pain like you've never imagined.

You rush over and push Steve to the ground, forcing him to roll the way every American school child learns as early as kindergarten. "Roll, Steve, roll to put it out," you yell.

Steve rolls all right—right into you. Your shirt catches easily, and you abandon Steve to figure it out for himself while you bat at the flames on your own clothing. You throw yourself on the ground and roll like mad; maybe you'll be a good example for Steve. The heat is unbearable, but when you look down a few minutes later the fire is out. Steve seems to have managed, too, though he's babbling constantly to himself.

The air is a little purer here, but now you've got to stand and get Steve back to safety. You crouch, trying to avoid the worst of the smoke, but you've been in it too long. You grow tired, and your chest feels like it is wrapped in steel bands. You can't catch your breath.

Steve crawls forward on his hands and knees, and doesn't even notice when you collapse behind him. You reach out and call "Steve, Steve," but your voice is barely a rasp.

You don't last much longer before the oxygen in your lungs is replaced with particulate-filled burning smoke.

THE END

This—this is all a little too much.

The front door isn't that far away. You can make it if you run, and then you'll be safe. You've had too many nightmares that end in burning buildings, no sir, no way.

You don't even hear the yells from your colleagues as you run for the door, arms up to shield your head. The smoke is thick, and it's hard to see, but you are running toward the light and don't care how much smoke you have to breathe as long as it means you get out.

It figures that this building didn't even bother to put in decent sprinklers. There aren't enough to keep you damp, much less to put out a fire. You vault over a chair that used to be an overstuffed purple lounger but is now a smoldering black block.

The glass in the front doors is broken—that's odd—but you turn sideways to dodge the sharpest slivers and then you're out!

You keep running a few steps backward, taking in deep breathes that make you cough the smoke back out of your lungs.

You're free! You're finally free of that place! Even without some kind of city-wide emergency, it'll be a good long while before they make you go back to work. You've dreamed of a day like this, even though you'll never say something that potentially incriminating to the police.

You watch as the flames climb higher, smoke now pouring out of the second story windows. Looking around, you hope that the fire department arrives soon so that more people can get out. There is an alternate stairway toward the back of the building—you tell yourself that the rest of your coworkers probably went out that way.

You begin walking. You're headed:

⊙ To Central Park. *Turn to page 136.*

⊙ Home. *Turn to page 75.*

What the heck—you have secretly harbored a firefighter fantasy since you were five and got to honk the horn during school fire safety day.

You grab the fire extinguisher outside the stairwell and yell, "Someone help me! There are people down here that need help!"

Bruce turns and runs upstairs; you think he's abandoned you, but he returns a moment later with an extinguisher, too. He must have gotten it from the next floor up.

"Becky! Call for help and get these people to safety," you call as you square your shoulders and step into the flames, not looking back to see if she bothered to listen to you.

You are completely unprepared for the heat, and it is ten times harder to breathe than you could have imagined. Coughing, you pull the trigger on your extinguisher, sweeping it in wide arcs to the left of the stairwell. Bruce starts in on the flames to the right.

You pull your shirt higher up over your nose and gesture toward the place where the front desk should be. Bruce nods that he understands and targets the bursts of flame climbing the walls.

You run to the front desk. The guard is slumped down, unresponsive. You pull on his arm, then lean down to check his pulse.

Your hand comes back sticky with blood. Crouched down near the floor, you stare at your hand in shock. Blood? No heartbeat?

How can you be the big hero now?

You see movement deeper in the smoke, so you run toward it, shooting flames with the foam from the extinguisher as you go. Around the corner, you find a group of people standing in a cluster, moaning and moving slowly.

"It's okay," you say, giving your best firefighter imitation. "We've called the fire department and are getting the fire under control. Come with me and we'll get you somewhere safer."

The people moan and shuffle their feet, barely walking toward you. "Come on, we need to hurry," you say, grabbing a middle-aged woman's arm.

Some of the skin from her wrist comes away at your touch. You stare up in horror at the group surrounding you.

So these must be those zombies they were talking about.

You and Bruce put out the flames, but you don't get time to relish your victory. You are consumed by another matter—or shall we say, monster—entirely.

THE END

Y̶ou haven't watched TV news in ages—the way the female anchors' hair is always exactly the same has always made you a little bit uncomfortable—so you have to hunt for the right channel.

A pert Hispanic woman is speaking intently, a low-grade of worry riding her voice.

"Reports are coming in from all across the city now," she says, holding a hand up to her ear as if listening. "People those who were infected earlier today are now up and moving. They are attacking indiscriminately. It is NOT, repeat NOT, safe to go outside."

"We received this image from New York University hospital earlier today," she says. An image of patients wearing those embarrassing no-back robes flashes on screen. They are moving toward the person holding the camera. Their eyes are wrong, and one man has a deep cut on his side, and you can see where he's pulling out the stitches with his movement. In the corner, you can just make out a doctor in blue scrubs screaming as he is bitten on the neck by an older woman.

"That hospital received the highest number of patients with this mystery illness, and this picture was taken about four hours after the CDC put the city on alert. We did not hear more from this tipster, but we believe—" the anchor pauses as if shocked by what she is about to say. "—We believe these people are behaving like—like zombies, for lack of a better term. It is further believed that infected individuals attack healthy people, as evidenced by this image." The screen zooms in to focus on the anguished doctor in the background.

When the camera refocuses on the anchor, she's stricken. "Lord have mercy on us all," she says, numbly.

You turn off the TV and

⊙ Call your best friend. You need to hear him tell you it'll all be okay. *Turn to page 154.*

⊙ Take a nap. Your head is spinning. Maybe if you close your eyes for a while it'll all turn out to be a bad dream. *Turn to page 77.*

The phone rings once.

"'Sup?"

"'Sup? Seriously? The world is ending or something and all you have to say is ''sup'? What is wrong with you, Adam?"

He sounds nonplussed. "Not like me freaking out is going to do much about it, is it?"

"You could maybe afford to freak out a little bit!" Your voice gets a teensy bit squeaky. Adam may not be afraid, but you sure as heck are. "What are you doing?"

"Just working and playing around on Facebook. There's this new game—"

"You are playing games and there are zombies coming to knock on your door and eat you at any minute? My God you really are crazy!"

"Look, calm down. It's not that big a deal. My door's locked, shades are closed, I'm sure it'll be fine. What else are we supposed to do now, anyway?" His commitment to unconcern is staggering.

"I dunno, fight, or panic, or something?"

"Yeah, those sound like they could kill me. I'll pass, thanks. But you can come over if you want or whatever."

You actually sputter for a moment. "Sppft sppttt!! The streets are filling with undead monsters and you want me to walk over there?!"

"Or don't. No big deal."

"You know, I called you because you're my best friend in the whole world and I'm kinda freakin' out and I thought maybe you'd have something reassuring or inspiring or whatever to say but I can see I was clearly wrong and I was expecting too much from you. Whatever. Bye."

You hang up and

⊙ Go to Adam's house. If you can't face down monsters with your best friend, what can you do? *Turn to page 84.*

⊙ Go sulk. *Turn to page 138.*

You cannot imagine how lucky you are. Sure, the world may be ending, but you just met the most beautiful human specimen you have ever seen.

"Hi there," you say, sitting next to her on the floor.

"Hey," she says.

"This whole thing is crazy, isn't it? It's insane how we could go from one day being normal people doing normal, everyday things, and the next, here we are, watching a broadcast about zombies walking our streets." You sigh for dramatic emphasis.

"I know," she says, sounding numb.

"There's so much of life I didn't get to experience, you know?" Time to start the waterworks. "I didn't even get to write a bucket list, much less cross things off it. I can't believe this could be the end!"

She looks at you for the first time, sympathy welling in her eyes. "Don't give up hope yet. We're still here."

She holds your hand, gently.

Your heart surges three times as fast. Oh wowza, she even has nice hands! Look at those manicured cuticles!

You look back into her eyes and sniffle, letting a tear fall down your cheek.

"Don't cry. It'll be okay," she says, pulling you to her shoulder. You sob quietly, snuggling into her bosom.

Sniff. "You smell good," you say, then suppress a giggle. Sniffle. "Hey, sorry for getting all emotional like that. Can we go somewhere a little more private?"

"Sure, absolutely," she says, and leads you into the maze of cubicles. "Be right back." She leaves you in a cube decorated in a tropical theme. It's a little sad.

She returns a moment later with a paper cup of water. "Here, you need to calm down a bit."

"Thanks," you say with a weak smile. "My hero." She smiles back.

"So what kind of things would you put on this bucket list of yours?" she asks.

"Oh, I dunno. See Tokyo, ride in a hot air balloon, pet a shark, eat real haggis, go to the moon." You stare up into her eyes. "Maybe make love to a beautiful stranger." You find yourself literally fluttering your eyelashes.

She smiles back at you. "Maybe that last one is on my list, too."

Forty-five minutes later, you've mangled the organization of a storage closet and crossed one thing off your bucket list.

You go back to your floor in a happy daze. You didn't even bother to learn her name.

⊙ *Turn to page 54.*

You cannot imagine how lucky you are. Sure, the world may be ending, but you met the most beautiful human specimen you have ever seen.

"Hi there," you say, sitting next to him on the floor.

"Hey," he says.

"This whole thing is crazy, isn't it? It's insane how we could go from one day being just normal people doing normal, everyday things, and the next, here we are, watching a broadcast about zombies walking our streets." You sigh for dramatic emphasis.

"I know," he says, sounding numb.

"There's so much of life I didn't get to experience, you know?" Time to start the waterworks. "I didn't even get to write a bucket list, much less cross things off it. I can't believe this could be the end!"

He looks at you for the first time, sympathy welling in his eyes. "Don't give up hope yet. We're still here."

He holds your hand, gently.

Your heart surges three times as fast. Oh wowza, he even has nice hands! Such lovely manicured cuticles!

You look back into his eyes and sniffle, letting a tear fall down your cheek.

"Don't cry. It'll be okay," he says, pulling you to his shoulder. You sob quietly, snuggling into his nice strong arms.

Sniff. "You smell good," you say, then suppress a giggle. Sniffle. "Hey, sorry for getting all emotional like that. Can we go somewhere a little more private?"

"Sure, absolutely," he says, and leads you into the maze of cubicles. "Be right back." He leaves you in a cube decorated in a winter wonderland theme. It's a little sad.

He returns a moment later with a paper cup of water. "Here, you just need to calm down a bit."

"My knight in shining armor," you say with a weak smile. He smiles back.

"So what kind of things would you put on this bucket list of yours?" he asks.

"Oh, I dunno. See Tokyo, ride in a hot air balloon, pet a shark, eat real haggis, go to the moon." You stare up into his eyes. "Maybe make love to a beautiful stranger." You find yourself literally fluttering your eyelashes.

He smiles back at you. "Maybe that last one is on my list, too."

Forty-five minutes later, you've mangled the organization of a storage closet and crossed one thing off your bucket list.

You go back to your floor in a happy daze. You didn't even bother to learn his name.

⊙ *Turn to page 54.*

Y ou cannot imagine how lucky you are. Sure, the world may be ending, but you met the two most beautifully formed people on earth.

You squeeze in between them, secretly rejoicing at the small bit of warm comfort you get from the contact with each of their legs, one on either side just barely brushing your own. In such close quarters, they can't give you any extra room. Pure bliss.

"So…" you start, eager for conversation with these two, "what do you up here?"

The man on your left says, "We're an ad agency. We do advertising." He says it as if to say you're probably a little slow.

You try again with the woman on your right. "Yeah, but what do you do?"

She barely glances at you, saying, "I do the art," and returning her gaze to the television, which seems to be showing some kind of report on explosions.

So your first gambit at conversation didn't go all that well. Okay. Try, try again.

"It kinda seems like maybe this is the end of the world," you say, quietly.

"Yeah," the man says. "How come all the Mayans and Nicodemuses or, heck, daily website horoscope-readers didn't give us a heads' up on this one?"

"It's just horrible," the woman says.

Seeing an opening, you hold her hand in yours. "It'll be okay," you say. A moment later, you also reach for the man's hand.

You introduce yourself in the same hushed tone. "I work downstairs."

Neither person does more than barely acknowledge you.

Well, you'll never get the answer you want if you don't try, so— "You know, if this really is the end of the world, why don't we go enjoy the last bit of our humanity?" you say to both, looking at each in turn. "Let's go out with a real bang, if you know what I mean."

For some reason, you managed to say this last part just as there is a lull on the television. Everyone in the room heard you; several people turn and stare.

The woman pulls her hand away from yours, disgusted. The man looks like he might punch you. He murmurs, "I think it's time for you to go."

Oh well, can't blame you for trying, can they?

You go back to your floor to report on what you've learned.

⊙ *Turn to page 54.*

You head up the stairs. At least you got the shorter route: you only have to explore six flights of stairs, but Becky's got at least 30-something. Sucker. Still, you're muttering about Bruce's lack of genitalia because he wouldn't let you take the elevator. As if you'd actually get trapped in there. Pfftt. Moron.

The next floor up is under construction, or was, anyway. As usual, the contractors must have called it quits early. You'd bet good money the building lockdown still counts as "billable hours." Sucks to be that owner. You see some tools, but mostly it's raw wood and plastic sheeting.

The next two stories are all one business, a janitorial supply company that recently went global. There are about sixty employees, some cleaning chemicals stacked up in boxes for shipment, but mostly the accountant and marketing types. They're quite friendly, enjoying cups of coffee and generally hanging out. You take your cup of joe, no creamer thanks, up to the next floor with you.

Floor 38 is a hodgepodge of small businesses. You've got a masseuse with a shady-looking table, a freelance writer operating out of what may have formerly been a closet, a paralegal—the only person who obeyed the mayor's orders, all the lawyers left hours ago—for a small firm specializing in divorces, and a couple of young kids who claim to own a technology start-up. Yeah right. They're nervous and fidgety, and have more or less been twiddling their thumbs since mid-afternoon. You send all of them downstairs to Bruce, where maybe their restless energy can at least be useful.

The thirty-ninth floor is home to the corporate offices of a fast-food chain you absolutely can't stand. Even their business office smells like grease and rat-droppings. You don't stay long.

Finally, you make it to the fortieth floor. It's a big-name advertising agency, and the walls are decorated with tasteful ads going back to the '50s. "Make your floors shine with ElectroShine!" The woman wielding the mop is honest-to-god wearing heels and pearls. Classy.

You swing open the glass doors and walk in. You can hear a TV in the background, and the sound of low voices, so you head that way. You're partway through the maze of cubicles when you're interrupted by a man's low bass.

"Can I help you with something?"

You back up to the offices you'd passed. They'd seemed empty, but now you can see a well-dressed Asian man. He looks dignified, even with his tie undone and loose around his neck. Judging by his office's view, he's the boss.

"Hi," you say, awkwardly. "I'm from floor 34. Just trying to get a sense of who all is in the building." You introduce yourself.

"Mr. Lee," Mr. Lee says, shaking your hand in return. "Seems our fair city is in a bit of dire straits."

"Yeah, it seems pretty crazy out there," you agree. You find that you're a little terrified of Mr. Lee, and you try to hide it. You're not doing well.

"Mm," Mr. Lee says.

"So, um, okay, so we're trying to come up with, like, a plan to defend the building and stuff," you say. Wow, you sure are eloquent. Best messenger ever.

"That so?" Mr. Lee says. He barely crooks an eyebrow.

"Yeah. So, you have any, like, supplies or anything that we can share?"

Mr. Lee rises from his cushy leather chair and walks toward the sound of the TV. Unsure of what's going on, you follow him.

"Can I get you a drink?" Mr. Lee asks, over his shoulder.

"Um, sure." You're hoping it's something stronger than fruit punch.

You come around the maze of blue cubicle walls and see a herd of employees, clothes rumpled from sitting on the floor, all staring at the large-screen television. It's showing the view from a TowerCam somewhere—there's a lot of smoke, and the streets are full of people, like New Year's Eve. The next shot is a zoomed-in look, maybe shot from inside a building, on the ground floor. Those definitely aren't New Year's revelers. More like Halloween, if everyone dressed as ambulatory crash victims. You shudder. The people on the floor continue to stare in numb silence.

"Yes, it looks pretty bad out there, doesn't it?" Mr. Lee says, noticing the direction of your gaze. "But you were asking about supplies. I suppose my helicopter on the roof counts, though it only seats a few. Other than that, I've got a bunch of artists, writers, a few managerial types, and this booze."

"Excuse me, what? Did you say 'helicopter'?" You're a bit flabbergasted. "On the roof?"

"Yes. But I believe I'll be using that mostly for me and perhaps a few others. Anyway, you're welcome to stay and enjoy my wet bar, as long as it lasts."

Mr. Lee has, evidently, dismissed you. He walks back to his office, swirling his scotch in the glass as he goes.

You:

◉ Are staying up here, with these people, and watching TV. At least here you don't have to work for Bruce. And there's a helicopter! *Turn to page 93.*

◉ Report back to Bruce. You are pretty sure Becky's not going to come back with any news as big as a helicopter. Ha-cha-cha you're in

161

business now! *Turn to page 167.*

"Okay. Good," you say, wiping your forehead with the back of your hand in a show of confident leadership you learned from one too many action movies. "Now we know the lay of the land. We can do this."

You are a lying wretch. You haven't got the slightest idea what you are going to do. You are making this all up completely off-the-cuff. But you sure as hell aren't going to stop now. It's the end of the world, and you've picked which horse you'll be riding into the sunset.

You start giving out orders—boom boom boom. Kristina's team is to consolidate food supplies at the cafeteria on floor eight, recruiting people from other floors as they go. Another team, spearheaded by Bruce, has the bigger job—deal with floor two.

It's now your way, or the highway—or rather, the now-completely deadlocked city street outside, but that didn't rhyme, did it?

You are going with Bruce's team. The mostly male band of eight or so arms themselves with whatever weaponry that can be fashioned out of office supplies. You're wielding the high-powered stapler (good for close combat) and a broom handle. Bruce has a pair of long kitchen knives. Others have broken a table and confiscated its legs.

You take the elevator down to the second floor, trying to maintain your tough exterior under the pinging elevator music in the cramped space. You actually snarl a bit when the doors open. You nod to the group behind you and step out.

The financial firm on floor two features a pale mint green lobby with expensive-looking couches. It's bereft of personality of any kind. An ominously dark-wood door on the right says "Conquest Capital" in gold lettering. You've found your target.

You and your band of merry men march up to the door. You indicate with a tuck of your head that everyone should lower their weapons. You're going to start with diplomacy.

But these financial types don't respect much except aggression, so you make sure everyone has their weapons at the ready.

You go in, your supporters filling in the tight hallway behind you.

There's no one at the heavy secretary's desk, so you continue into the offices, monuments of glass and money. Your little band of Jets comes face-to-face with the Sharks, dressed in sharp expensive suits and ties.

Perhaps after this you'll upgrade your wardrobe.

The man at point among the financial executives is devilishly handsome with eyes you are working hard to consider cruel. It's just not fair that he's both rich and has the looks from a high-fashion men's catalog. You grip your stapler a little harder.

"Hello," you say. "We're from floor 34. We're working out a plan to secure the building, because it looks like we're on our own this time." You pause for effect.

"I hear you didn't approve of my messengers before." You glance at Bruce, his muscled arm bulging now that his shirt is torn.

The incredibly handsome rich bastard sneers. "We don't want to work with you or anyone else," he says. "We here at Conquest know how to manage a crisis just fine, thank you."

Hm. You hadn't really thought this part through. You had sort of hoped Bruce was wrong about this whole thing and that these people would happily join your group. Well, if wishes were fishes, you'd be enjoying a fourteen-course seafood dinner right now instead of preparing a goddam office building for the end of the world. That's life for you.

"We've secured the cafeteria on floor eight. If you don't join us, we'll leave you here, without supplies. That might be unpleasant for you," you say, hoping your uncertainty hasn't leaked into your voice.

"I think we'll probably manage."

Damn. This guy could be James Bond's evil twin. He even has the watch.

He probably has the car, too. Some guys have all the luck.

"Fine, if that's the way you want it. Good luck," you say, and begin to turn to leave.

Just then, the power goes out, with a bang you can feel shivering up your legs. That can't be good.

"Well shit," someone says behind you. You can't help but agree.

"Hey fellas," you call out to the financial types. "Any of you got glow sticks or something? We'd like to return to our own floor. Preferably without breaking legs or anything."

Your only response is an exaggerated sigh and the sound of very expensive shoes walking away.

"Well, come on guys, we'll manage on our own," you say. "Hey, Nick, be really careful with those knives, okay? You practically stabbed Becky on the ride down. And remember, they're like scissors—carry them point-down this time, yeah?"

"Oh, right," Nick says.

You are feeling your way along the hall when a light shows up behind you. The Secret Agent guy has a flashlight so big it could murder someone.

"Hey, thanks," you say, and reach out to take it.

"Um, no," he says, pulling it back out of your way. "I'll merely be escorting you part of the way. This flashlight belongs to Conquest, thankyouverymuch."

Dick.

"Fine. Thanks anyway," you say. You let Dick McDickerson go first, so he can show you where the stairs are. They're around a corner, behind a less-impressive wood door. Man, this is going to be a long walk. Why couldn't your office be on floor four or something?

"Hey, what's that sound?" Nick says, just before you reach the door. Everyone stops to listen. "Do you hear voices?"

Dick the SuperDick gives a half-shrug and opens the door.

The beam from the flashlight reveals several seriously mutilated faces, ripped clothing, and blank eyes. A woman with her hair matted to her face with blood moans, a low guttural sound.

"These people need serious medical help!" you say.

Or you would have said, had you not been cut off halfway as they surged through the open door and right into Richard-better-known-as-Dickface.

He was tackled like the last hot toy at a holiday super-sale, if sales included more blood and teeth-gnashing. As it was, the guy from Conquest Capital got to see if his expensive flashlight really could be used as a murder weapon. He desperately smashed the light at the heads of his attackers, sending the beam flashing madly.

You're only a bit ashamed to say it took a good ten seconds for anyone in your group to do anything. Perhaps they weren't deliberately holding back. Perhaps they were stunned that a guy they just met was being eaten alive by zombies.

Perhaps.

His screams galvanized the group into action, everyone hacking and beating and kicking the monstrous people. They seemed to have no regard for self-preservation, but they also weren't particularly intelligent, which is the only way you probably survived. You don't know how long the fight actually lasted, but it seemed interminable. The last time you were in a real fight was…the seventh grade, and that ended as soon as the other kid hit you hard enough that you fell on your butt.

There weren't any teachers to intercede now.

It didn't matter, though. Your group managed to hack and slash the attackers—one got kicked all the way back down the stairs—but it was too late for the man you had briefly known as Dick. His remains are gruesome, and you feel like maybe you'll puke. You pick up the flashlight instead, shining it at your companions. A few minor wounds, but nothing terrible. You'll recover.

"Well," is all you say.

You take your team back into the Conquest Capital office, explain what happened. They are disbelieving at first, but one display of the tortured bodies in the hallway is enough to convince the others that maybe joining you is a pretty good idea after all. Which works out well for you;

they have a small stash of guns. Apparently the owner is a bit paranoid about being robbed.

Over the next hours, days, and weeks, you lead the population of your tower to defend your ground. The first floor is considered a total loss: too many glass doors are smashed in by the undead attackers. But with the help of the Conquest group—now known as the Conquistadors, for their collective bravery in the face of gruesome odds—you defend the building from the second floor up. The power doesn't come back on, but you have a few engineers from the tech startup on floor five who got sufficiently bored to build a little generator, enough to cook some food. You orchestrate the removal of mirrors from the bathrooms to help reflect sunlight through strategically smashed windows, granting at least some light to the dark building. At night, you burn a small fire on each floor.

You survive. There are losses, of course—Becky died screaming when a horde of zombies jumped her at her post on the second floor—but unexpected victories, too—Nick finds a place of strength he didn't know he had in him, and his help is crucial to your rise to power.

It's not much, but you've got your very own fiefdom now. You rule as fairly and wisely as you are able, eventually setting up a throne room on the top floor. You like the view.

All Hail the Great Ruler of Tower 2415.

THE END

Y ou return to Bruce, still in the workroom, reporting back everything you've learned.

"Oh yeah, and the ad agency on the fortieth floor also has a helicopter on the roof." You say this as if it were an unimportant afterthought, and are gratified when Bruce's eyes go big.

"A what? A helicopter?" he says, his voice changing from surprised to contemplative. "That's useful. Good job."

You beam in his praise. Ha-cha-cha indeed.

When Becky gets back, Bruce listens carefully, but it's pretty clear he's already got his mind made up, so it's unsurprising when he says, "well, I've got a plan. We're going to perform a takeover of the helicopter on the roof. It's our only way outta here."

He sounds so confident and manly and awesome. And now you're definitely his favorite.

"What do we do, Bruce?" you ask.

"We'll start by asking Mr. Lee nicely. Maybe he'll be reasonable," Bruce pauses dramatically, looking around at the gathered group. "And, if not, we take it by force."

Now we're talkin'.

Bruce sketches out his plan. Becky will stay behind, defending floor thirty-four's position and serving as ambassador to any of the other floors that also want to build themselves barricades based on the templates your floor created. You and most of the others will go with Bruce, as his backup envoys to floor forty.

Not half an hour later, you're upstairs, again facing Mr. Lee. Bruce says, "Nice to meet you, Mister Lee. I've enjoyed the work your agency has done over the years. That commercial with the tap-dancing dogs? Golden, if you'll pardon the pun, sir."

"Thank you," Mr. Lee says, not even cracking a smile. "I assume you and your people have not come up here merely to compliment my work?"

"No sir, I'm afraid not," Bruce says. "I've come here to ask to borrow your helicopter. It is probably our only way out of here."

"Hmm," Mr. Lee says. "And why should I give you my very expensive flying machine rather than riding it to safety myself?"

"Because," Bruce says, flexing his arms menacingly, "I'm prepared to take it one way or another."

"Mm. I see," Mr. Lee says. His face doesn't reflect a trace of intimidation. "Well, come into my office then. We'll discuss this privately."

You look at Bruce uneasily—after all, this could be a trap!—but he nods and follows Mr. Lee into the office. The door clicks in place in your face. You and the others stare into the glass-enclosed room as Mr. Lee walks to his chair and sits, Bruce takes a seat in the leather chairs in front of the desk. Mr. Lee pushes a button on the desk, and the glass fogs up instantly. All you can see are vague man-shaped blurs. After a while, your feet hurt, so you slump to the floor, leaning against the walls. The assembled group of backup envoys is too nervous to talk much.

Some time later, Bruce opens the door. "Not to worry, folks, we've got a plan. Mr. Lee and I here are going to go with the pilot and find help—probably there are Army Reserves not too far away—and then we'll come back."

Bruce turns to face you directly. "I'm putting you in charge while I'm gone," he says.

"I-" you gulp. "I thought we were taking the helicopter."

Bruce slaps one of his big paws on your shoulder. "This is better for all of us," he says jovially. "We'll be back lickety-split, you'll see. And we'll save everyone else in the building. You just have to keep this place safe in the meantime. Okay?"

"Okay." You're not really sure this is okay, but you're unable to come up with a better response.

Bruce, Mr. Lee, and a red-haired pilot lead the way to the roof. You and your band of envoys follow, huddling near the door as the blades begin to whoosh whoosh whoosh. You watch with fear in your throat as Bruce climbs in and the helicopter lifts off.

"I'm sure they'll be back before nightfall," you say.

Neither the helicopter, nor Bruce, nor anyone else comes back, and it turns out you're shit at running a building. No one accepts your authority, and barely six hours have passed before the barricades are broken down. By the time the power goes out, you have completely lost control. There's a brawl with the employees of floor forty over the alcohol, and after that's drunk, at least a few people try out the cleaning supplies, hoping for something, at least, to dull the pain of existence. It doesn't work, and you're left with the unpleasant job of dragging bodies down the stairs.

It's pure anarchy. You manage to keep the building free of zombies, except for a few incursions, and everyone is safe from those monsters as long as they stay on floors six or above. But that's no protection from the monsters you've got trapped in the building with you—office workers driven insane by hunger and fear are not a pretty sight.

When a fire starts—probably in the basement or first floor somewhere, you aren't sure if it was set or an accident—all is lost. Those who don't die of smoke inhalation or in the flames themselves throw themselves off the building. Those on the lower floors sometimes survive, only to be dragged into the crowd of zombies and eaten. You can hear the screams echoing up the building.

You can't handle that kind of death, and you're afraid of falling anyway. You lock yourself inside an office and breathe deeply until your throat burns and your eyes water. If you're lucky, the smoke will kill you before the flames.

THE END

"This is great, Douglass. You and me, we're gonna save everyone in this building. We've got everything we need to get outta here alive. You with me?"

"Sure, I guess." Douglass's enthusiasm is less than stellar, but he's all you've got. He'll have to do.

You explain your plan to Douglass, and he nods in all the right places. He asks a few questions, but nothing you can't answer. Good.

Outside the glass windows, you see more and more people walk by. By now you have no doubt that Douglass is right about the zombies: they don't look right. It's either a zombie uprising or the general fashion sense of New York has suddenly hit bottom: the walkers are bloodied, with ripped clothing, bad hair, and missing shoes. They walk without purpose. Every so often, one slams into the glass window and ricochets, leaving slimy bloody imprints, like a hawk chasing its own reflection at full speed.

Douglass hits a grey nondescript button on his security desk and speaks into the microphone, sending his voice echoing into every office on every floor.

"Hello ladies and gentlemen. This is Douglass at the front desk. As you probably know by now, we got a problem. Our buildin' is under attack by zombies."

"Let me say that again. New York City is facing an honest-to-God zombie uprisin'."

You give Douglass a thumbs-up.

"If everyone would please make their way calmly down the stairs to the lobby, we have a plan of action to get us all outta here. Bring only what you can carry easily. And also anythin' that you maybe could use as a weapon. Oh, and if those of you nearby could stop at the thirty-fifth floor and mebbe pick up some tools or lumber or whatever, that would be great. Thanks!"

"Good job, Douglass, real good." You give him a hearty slap on the shoulder. "Think they'll listen to you?"

"Mebbe, mebbe not. But I think we got a good plan, so it was worth askin' them," Douglass says with a shrug.

People start coming down the stairs a few minutes later, beginning with those on the lowest floors. They look equal parts bemused, bewildered, and scared. As people arrive, you explain your plan and set people to work. You take a crew of twelve or so down to the basement, leaving Douglass to greet and assemble everyone else. Little by little, though, they are coming.

The basement is in desperate need of a thorough cleaning, but thankfully it is at least well-lit. There is a lot of electrical cord, some wood, and several kinds of tools. You and your helpers grab anything that looks remotely useful. By the time you've carried up an armful, Douglass has recruited more people to haul things out of the basement, so the stairs become populated with a regular stream of people moving up and down with arms heavy laden or sleeves rolled up for more.

There's a good crowd by now, and several people with experience in construction or woodworking or whatever, so you hand off the building to them. You focus on explaining the general idea of the plan.

A few people think you're a moron, that's true, and if they still think that after watching zombies ping off the windows, well, then, they're pretty much lost causes. You and Douglass wish them well and send them back up the stairs to figure out how they're going to handle this on their own.

After about forty-five minutes, Douglass points out a figure in a slim suit. You give him the thumbs-up again and stride over to talk to Mr. Lee.

"And so that's why we'd like your help, sir," you say, having explained your plan for the hundredth time. "If you could take your helicopter, sir, and act as our navigator, I think we could get a lot more people out of here safely."

Mr. Lee is stern and unreadable. He looks you up and down, judging, before finally saying, "Okay. I will get my pilot. Have Douglass call when he'd like us to take off, will you?" Mr. Lee turns on a well-shined heel and walks to the elevator.

"Thank you, sir!" you call after him. You can't believe it. Now your plan might actually work!

It takes another two hours of relentless whirring drills and hammering nails, and not a few panic attacks among the gathered officefolk, but eventually you're ready to go. Douglass has organized the groups by general office size, each group arranged in a flying V, with those on the outer edges wielding wooden or metal or plastic (or whatever else you could find) shields. People inside are given weapons of whatever kind; mostly heavy pipes or sharpened sticks, but also a few nail guns, a flare gun, and, from one particularly enthusiastic floor, a homemade flamethrower (Douglass wouldn't let them test it inside the building, though, so who knows if that one will do anything).

Douglass has been listening to news reports all this time, and it's from him that you get your destination: police have blocked off all the bridges. If there's any way off Manhattan Island, that's where you'll need to go.

Mr. Lee's pilot, a smiling red-headed woman, brought you a walkie-talkie. It's all you carry as you take your place in the middle of the first V. You give Douglass the nod, and he makes the call.

Your group heads outside. Here goes nothing.

At first, progress is seamless. The walkers don't seem to notice you at all, and you get the whole first group out without incident. You're waving the next group out when a walker, still pushing his hot dog cart, swivels toward the group.

"Remember what we talked about! Hold the shield wall! Second row, use your weapons!"

The hot dog cart slams into the group, breaking a hole in the line. A man from the third floor, the hibachi school, starts taking wide slashes at the walker, connecting with a solid THWACK with each swing. The hot dog cart slams on its side, squishing the leather-clad foot of one of the shield-holders. He hops around in loud pain, and other walkers, as if sensing weakness, come shuffling forward.

"Back in line! Back IN LINE!" you holler, and Squished Toes notices just in time. He brings his wooden shield up as a walker lunges at him, and he falls back into the supporting arms of the rest of the V. There's a short struggle until a nail-gun-wielder makes a good hit, but the line holds.

The radio crackles. "We're up," says the helicopter pilot, and you hear the steady thud-thud-thud far overhead. "Looks like the road ahead is reasonably clear. Get those groups moving."

Little by little, you get each group out, about 135 people all told. A few who rejected your plan initially try to bolt the other direction, and their screams echo up the eerily quiet sidewalk, sending a shiver through the armored escape groups.

Your uncanny parade continues its grim march toward the bridge. They're no military force, and there are a few injuries along the way, but Mr. Lee's Eyes in the Sky give you a decent warning of trouble, and you make steady progress.

By the time you reach sight of the bridge, Mr. Lee must have notified the police of your coming. Troops in full armor or police riot gear come out to greet you, shooting walkers with decisive rat-tat-tat's from their assault weapons.

By God, you've made it.

A month later, you and Douglass are greeted by the President at the White House. Thanks to your actions, the majority of your officemates made it out alive—the largest group to escape the Manhattan death trap. Though the military was eventually sent in, there were few other survivors. You are given a Medal of Honor, and your smiling mug is plastered on every news outlet in America and internationally.

Congratulations, hero.

THE END

"Woo!" you yell, triumphant. "I can't believe we did that! That was incredible!"

Your glee is uncontainable.

"I know!" Adam says. "Holy crap, I thought we were done for for a second there!"

"Whew, I know," you say.

"Hey look, more are coming," Adam says, gesturing up the road with a tilt of his chin.

"Wanna waste 'em?" you say.

Adam hefts his lamp pole. "Let's do this."

The two of you stride out to meet the incoming shufflers. They appear to be a mix of midday shoppers—a business man in a suit, a young-twenties woman with "Store Associate Kathy" on a bright pin attached to her red polo shirt, a soccer mom with a too-perky ponytail, and a dejected-looking short man in his thirties with an entirely inappropriate mustache. You can practically hear the whispers of the neighbors. They may all be too scared to go outside, but not you. You are awesome. Pure awesome.

Adam lays into the zombies with a massive swat from the lamp pole, which bends from the sheer force and the impact against dense zombie heads. You throw a knife, aiming for that cool spinning trick, but it lands harmlessly at a zombie's feet. It doesn't even notice when it kicks it aside, shuffling closer to you. Damn it. That could have been so cool.

Adam glances at you and shrugs. His metal pole has broken into two pieces, which he's trying to use as oversized dueling sticks. He's not doing well, so you step in, swinging your golf club, which connects with the scalp of the soccer mom with a meaty THWACK while he switches to his whiffle bat. It suddenly doesn't seem like such a good weapon.

You're getting tired. This zombie-fighting stuff is serious work.

"Hey—" you pant to Adam as you dodge the mustache's lurch. "Can—we—maybe," you gasp for a second, "go back—in?"

"Definitely," Adam says. He's given up the whiffle bat—the Store Associate zombie bit it and wrested it out of his grasp. He's down to the Taser and looking alarmed.

Assessing the situation, you decide it's time for fire. Adam gives you a nod.

You click on the flame, then pull the trigger on the air freshener. A jet of flame leaps five feet in front of you, melting the face off the businessman. The other zombies catch fairly quickly, too.

You and Adam turn and run back to the house.

The zombies do not die as you expected. No. Now they are both zombies and ON FIRE. Their hair burns first, making them look like melting cancer patients for a second, then their clothes catch, and finally their skin. The whole time, they shuffle after you.

You think you're safe once you're behind the door, but the zombies pound on the walls, the flames dripping off their bodies.

Adam's brownstone was built in the 1890s. His parents bought it for him to encourage him to move out of their house; an exorbitant gift to some, but small potatoes from his background.

It burns like a bonfire.

And you are the marshmallow.

It took out four other houses on the block, too, because the fire department isn't exactly in a hurry to fight flames in the midst of a zombie uprising.

Sucks for the neighbors.

THE END

The bile rises in your stomach and you lean over, bracing yourself against your knees as you dry-heave against the brick wall.

"Hey, are you okay?" Adam says, resting a hand on your shoulder.

You turn to glare at him as you wipe the mess from your mouth. The smell of vomit combined with the bloody ichor is almost enough to make you sick again. "Am I OKAY?" you holler. "Am I goddamn okay? Are you serious, man? That was awful! We almost died! And we're completely outnumbered. Those used to be PEOPLE, dammit. That girl, that girl right there used to just go about her day, checking people out at a store, and now she's some awful monster and I stabbed her in the eye because she tried to eat me. I COULD NOT BE MORE UN-OKAY!"

Adam looks chagrined, his shoulders slumping forward. "Yeah, you're right. We're in a nightmare and I don't know the way out."

You take a deep breath, trying to calm yourself though your mind continues reeling in hysteria. "Okay. Okay, we were nearly massacred out here..." you start, then glance up the street. Your shouting has attracted attention from the neighbors; zombies, lots of them, are hobbling your way. "Um..." you say. "Adam, I think we need to go inside. NOW."

Hearing your tone, Adam glances over his shoulder. "Shit," he mutters and backs toward the door.

If you have anything going in your favor, it's that the zombies are slow. You're a little ways away from the door, but the adrenaline churning through your system sends you hurtling back up the stairs after Adam. You slam the door shut as the first undead creature stumbles against the bottom step.

"Crap, that was close," Adam says.

"Too close," you agree. The panic is still throbbing under your skin, making your vision go wonky. You shake your head. "Quick, we've got to barricade the door again."

In a few minutes, your makeshift barricades are back in place, just in time for the scratching of fingernails to begin outside, the moans an eerie mantra from outside.

"We can't be that stupid again," you sigh. You've slid down to lean against the wall, holding your head in your hands.

There's a thump against the door, hard enough to rattle the picture on the wall behind you. "But we can't stay here forever, either," Adam says.

You stare at him despairingly. "What are we gonna do?"

It seems impossible now. It was weird at first, then a little scary, like a horror movie with bad special effects. Then it got to be a little exciting, you putting yourself into the movie as the hero. But the truth is, you're no hero and there's no triumphant ending you can see. It's overwhelming and your breath begins to come in great shuddering sighs.

Adam sniffles. "Don't give up yet," he says, giving the pep talk that you both have seen in a hundred action movies but don't really believe now. "We'll…we'll figure it out. We can do this," he says. But his eyes look doubtful.

The courage and panic makes your chest feel tight. You cling to that feeling, to that hope, like the safety bar on a rollercoaster that's going too fast. "Sure, you're right. We can do this," you say, clutching his hand and giving it a squeeze.

You each go and clean off the ick that came from fighting the zombies. The water feels cool against your skin and makes you feel real: real, and alive, and sadly not trapped in a nightmare.

No one really tells you how much of handling a disaster is waiting.

Waiting for something to happen, for someone to come along and fix it, waiting for it to be over. You and Adam find yourselves sitting together at the darkened dining table, all the windows and doors blocked up, eating chips and stale Twinkies while the undead rattle and grunt at the doors. It's so surreal you have trouble believing it, but a glance at Adam confirms it is: you both have the same exhausted, dead-eyed stare, the same feelings of oppressive panic. You feel like you need to do something but can't figure out anything that would help. You take down and rebuild your tower of snack food.

"We need to find out what is going on outside," Adam says slowly, between bites of chip. His mouth is orange with flavor dust.

"Yeah, okay," you say, stacking another mini-cake on your tower.

"Find me some batteries, I think I have an old weather radio in here somewhere," he says, sliding out of his chair. Mutely, you dig through the supplies on the table. As he leaves the room, you choke back a yell: don't leave me, you want to yell, god please don't make me do this alone! But then he's back, the radio in his hand, and it's okay again.

You hand over the batteries and Adam fiddles with the knobs, seeking out a station. Finally, one comes in, fuzzy at first, but then clearer:

"—PROTECT YOURSELF FROM THE ATTACKERS. IT IS VERY IMPORTANT TO REMEMBER…" The radio hits a burst of static. "THE FOLLOWING IS AN EMERGENCY BROADCAST FOR THE NEW YORK CITY AREA, INCLUDING QUEENS, NEW YORK, KINGS, RICHMOND, NASSAU, AND SUFFOLK—"

The robotic voice is oddly soothing, a reminder that you're not delusional, that this is really happening…that there are others out there who may be able to help.

You and Adam listen to the drone at low-volume. It offers little useable advice, but you feel better. You sit back in your chair, focusing on the lull of the voice over the moans of the monsters outside.

A harsh BLEEEP BLEEEEEP interrupts your reverie:

"THIS IS AN EMERGENCY BROADCAST. PLEASE LISTEN FOR THE FOLLOWING EMERGENCY MESSAGE," the robot says. You wish you had that kind of calm under pressure.

The robotic man's voice is replaced by an announcer, a woman who sounds like vaguely like a news reporter who used to do the traffic updates. She says, "Attention all residents of New York. If there is anyone, anyone still alive in there, we're doing what we can."

There is a pause. You sit up straighter, staring at Adam. She comes back; you can hear her deep breath before she speaks again. "We have limited options for evacuation, however, it is imperative that you do evacuate if you are able. Any humans able to walk or otherwise safely move about, head toward any of the bridges to the mainland. Identify yourself clearly; a sign may help. Repeat, head to the mainland. Soldiers there will clear you for reentry."

"What are we supposed to do, walk through hordes of zombies?" Adam says, disgustedly.

"Listen, maybe there's more," you say, but you don't mean it. There is no way you can make it from Adam's house all the way to the bridge. Not through that horde hammering on the walls.

"We realize not everyone may be able to make this exit," the traffic reporter-turned-emergency-broadcaster says. "Stay tuned for further instructions."

BLEEP BLEEEP. The radio blared its signal and returned to the regular droning.

"There's no way we can do that," you say quietly.

Adam nods.

"I guess there isn't anything we can do except wait."

Several hours later, the radio is starting to give you a headache. In the dark of night, zombies had broken the glass in one window, and one—a balding black man with blood oozing out of both eyes—had managed to get its head inside before Adam could beat it with a hammer. Now it hung limply, just inside the windowsill, dripping black liquid down the wall.

"Let's move upstairs," you said after that, and Adam had agreed. Laboriously, you hauled all the supplies up the stairs. You're exhausted, and Adam doesn't look much better, but you're afraid to sleep. Just after you get everything resettled in the hallway upstairs, the weather radio blares again:

BEEEP BLEEEEP

"Attention, attention, anyone still alive in the New York City area." The female announcer is back, and she sounds as exhausted as you feel.

"Black Hawk helicopters will be making a sweep of the city at daybreak. Repeat, military helicopters will make a sweep of the city at daybreak to find any survivors. If possible, make way to a balcony or rooftop so that you can be seen. Rescues will be attempted where possible. Repeat…"

You look up at Adam and manage half a grin. "That's it then," you say. "We've just got to make it until morning."

"Hallelujah," Adam says weakly. He grins, lopsided. "Just until morning."

You lean against each other, and unintentionally fall into a light doze. It's the sleep of the overstressed; tense, but about nothing. It's a reassuring mindlessness after the day's terrors.

The thump of helicopters wakes you. Light is barely visible through the window. "Adam, Adam, wake up! They're coming!" you say, shaking him.

He blinks and rouses himself, grabbing the hammer with both hands, looking for the threat.

"No, no, the helicopters, man, the helicopters! We made it! We're gonna get out of here!" You whoop in happiness, a delirious grin spreading across your face.

"Hell yeah—" Adam says.

A calamitous CRACK sounds from downstairs.

"Shit, I think they are coming too!" he says.

You lean over the bannister. He's right: the zombies have gotten in, broken through the window completely. They're climbing over each other, heads swiveling until unseeing eyes find you.

"Shitshitshitshit," you yell. "We've got to get out of here, now!"

Adam nods and throws himself toward an open doorway. It's his spare bedroom, which you've never been in before, and it looks like he's barely seen it, too; all too-neat bedspreads and extra cardboard boxes, never unpacked. He hurtles toward the window, straining to lift it.

"Come on, come on," you say.

"Painted…shut…" he says, his arms bulging with effort. Behind you, the third stair creaks. They're climbing. You don't know how, but they are.

Sliding in next to Adam, you both pull against the window, pull pull pull, until finally, a crack and it budges. The window is old glass, unused to movement, and it groans as you rattle it open.

From the doorway, a zombie moans in return.

"OHshitohshitohshit," you say, scrambling out the window. The roof is steeply slanted, but you don't care, you have to move, and your fingers scrabble for purchase on the thin tiles. "Adam, come on!" you scream, and your best friend in the world rushes out the window, just in time, just barely in time. The snapping teeth of a 15-year-old in a schoolgirl outfit follow close behind.

You climb up the roof, panting, your fingers bleeding from the textured tiles.

There, in the near distance, are two huge thumping helicopters. You stand and wave your arms.

They see you, and come your way. You're saved. You're going to make it out of here.

The Eastern Seaboard is shuttered, city by city, but the containment measures put in place in New York seem to hold, so much of the mainland is preserved. Those who don't make it to a helicopter are doomed, though a few pathetic stragglers do make it to the military firing line on the bridges. The disease wraps the nation in fear for a few months, until the next celebrity wrongdoing distracts the populace.

But you never forget. You remain one of the hallowed few, the zombie survivors. It's something you'll tell your grandchildren about during school assemblies.

CONGRATULATIONS, YOU SURVIVED.

THE END

Section Z

You're a zombie now.

Of course, you don't actually know you're a zombie, because you don't know much of anything anymore, but you are. The upside is that all your troubles, anxieties, and worries are gone—forever.

Oh, and you're alive!

Kinda.

Sorta.

In a manner of speaking, anyway.

But whatever did you in would, under typical circumstances, have killed you in a way that did not bring you back, and yet here you are, eyes more or less open again, stumbling on along this journey called—er…well, not life, exactly, but…well, you get the idea.

———

You thrash around, limbs reluctant to move properly. You move, not paying any particular attention to your surroundings. You shuffle as you walk, slowly and aimlessly. Sometimes you moan, but it's just another sound.

It is challenging to keep your head upright. You continually try anyway, but more often than not, your head rests against a shoulder or, sometimes, tips all the way back.

After walking this way for a time, you become aware of other movements around you. There is more moaning now, and you sometimes bump into the other moving things. Once, you walk directly into the moaning thing in front of you, and reflexively bite, ripping flesh away with a yank of your teeth.

Fluid drips down your jaw. The other thing—another zombie, it turns out—moves away, continuing its own shuffling walk, but does not react otherwise. A few minutes later, it falls. The other moving things move around or over it.

You reach a barrier and cannot move forward. You:

⊙ Turn this way. *Turn to page 183.*

⊙ Turn thattaway. *Turn to page 185.*

⊙ Stare at the wall, swaying slightly. *Turn to page 186.*

Y ou shift directions—something you would consider a feat if you had enough mental capacity left to consider anything. You don't congratulate yourself on your independent thought. You shuffle onward.

You are the definition of aimless.

You walk with your mindless peers, milling about on the pavement. Sometimes you collide with a parked vehicle; sometimes you remember to turn around them. You walk into a taxi's side mirror with enough force to break it off the car, leaving a two-inch indention in your side. That probably should have hurt. You moan a little. You limp a bit more heavily.

There's motion up ahead. Your head lolls forward, showing your interest. You stare out of the side of one eye in the direction of the movement, though it was likely just another of your zombie brethren falling into a manhole.

But no! There's the motion again. It's moving much faster than the other zombies. You shuffle forward a bit more eagerly—which is to say, at exactly the same pace, but with a slight sense of purpose. You moan in excitement: "Aaauuugghhhhh."

If you had retained cognition, you would notice that there are actually two things creating the movement. You could have speculated that the man, of moderate fitness and dressed in what used to be an expensive shirt and tie with dress slacks, might be the father of the little blonde girl he has by the hand, her pigtails bouncing as he darts from hiding place to hiding place dragging her along, half-carrying her. She looks about one-and-a-half, with cute-as-pie squishy cheeks and an overstuffed unicorn tucked under her arm. The man looks afraid, and the girl looks as if she recently woke from a nap.

But you're a zombie now, so all you think is "BrrAAIINnnNS."

(Actually, that is kind of a complex thought for you in your current state, but it's close enough).

The father is trying to go unnoticed behind a garbage bin, but you aren't the only undead to see the pair. A group is starting to gather closer. The father notices, and panics. He leaps up and pulls on the handle of the nearest car, a beat-up blue compact. Though he pulls frantically, it's locked. He pauses, reaching in his pocket, daughter balanced on his opposite hip. She's starting to look more alert, eyes darting from one shuffling monster to the next.

The man finds the ring of keys, but his hands are shaking. A short, round zombie flails an arm at them, and the father pulls away, barely far enough to stay out of reach. He presses himself against the car. The girl starts to cry; he's shoved her in his haste.

You shuffle closer. You can practically feel the two heartbeats now. You're nearly in reach.

You:

⊙ Reach for the man. *Turn to page 190.*

⊙ Grab the girl. *Turn to page 192.*

⊙ Bang on the vehicle. *Turn to page 194.*

Y ou sorta-kinda hit the impediment at a slight angle, so it can't so much be said that you chose to turn aside as that it happens to be convenient.

But that doesn't matter, does it? Either way, you have changed directions, and now you're shuffling off to face your destiny. Pretty powerful stuff, destiny, even if it does only feel like a stutter-step shuffle down the street with a bunch of other mindless monsters—because, well, it is.

At any rate, there you go, a-shufflin' down the street.

Zombies don't have a sense of time, so you don't know how long you've been wandering, but it is long enough that your hind foot is dragging behind you a little more steadily than before.

Up ahead, you hear an odd noise. It's a low vibrato sound that you can feel in your loosely pounding chest. You turn toward it, interested in this new stimuli.

Let's call it the Call of the Wild.

You walk toward the sound, and now hear others as well. Besides the roar, you hear squawking and screeching. If you could read, you'd know that the arch you pass under says "Central Park Zoo." But you can't, so you continue onward, as zombies are wont to do.

This place is amazing. You can feel so many heartbeats—big ones, little ones, fast ones. The roaring sound comes again, and you shamble toward it.

It's coming from a really big furry beast. The sight of it makes you salivate. You want to chomp chomp chomp it. But you can't get to it; something is in your way. You're leaning against a low iron fence. The lion is below you, in a pit surrounded by a gully.

Looking around, you also notice many tiny heartbeats coming from a place nearby. That's pretty exciting, too.

You:

⊙ Go for the lion. It's right there, after all. *Turn to page 215.*

⊙ Many is better than one, you think—or would, if you still had cognition. *Turn to page 219.*

You stare at the barrier. You sway. Sometimes a bit of your lip gets caught in your teeth, but after that happens a few times it doesn't happen any more because you've chewed your lips off. There's not enough blood left in you to really bleed.

Something bumps you, and you hit the barrier, opening another wound in the flesh that used to be your face. It also jostled you to the ground. You stand, after a moment, and if you still had the capacity for feelings you might have been surprised the barrier is no longer blocking you.

You shuffle forward again, back into the flow of moving things that do not have heartbeats.

There is less light after a time, but you do not stop. There is no reason. You shuffle forward.

There is a sound somewhere in front of you. It is a squeak, high-pitched. You keep walking slowly. The darkness gets darker. You are going down, and it gets colder, but you do not mind. You keep moving.

You hear the squeak again.

You:

⦿ Walk toward the sound. *Turn to page 187.*

⦿ Just keep moving. *Turn to page 188.*

You amble slightly toward the squeaking sound. There is also a rustling sound, but your ears can no longer hear it. It is the sound of many small feet.

You continue walking toward the place where you heard the sound. You take a step forward—and there is no step in front of you.

You fall. Something inside you has broken. You can no longer stand on your legs. No matter. You pull yourself forward with your arms. There is more squeaking nearby. You move more slowly now, pulling yourself along, legs dragging uselessly. Something crawls over you.

If you could still feel your legs, you might have felt that you are being bitten by small razor-sharp teeth, but you do not. You continue crawling forward. Something else crawls over you, and again you are bitten.

You crawl forward, and your hand lands on something fuzzy and warm. It has a heartbeat. It is squeaking. You are compelled to bring the thing to your mouth. It shrieks now. It is wiggling in your hand, and nearly escapes, but you have a strong grip. You take a large bite out of it. Even with grievous injury, it continues to struggle. You bite it again. It stops moving.

Its compatriots do not mourn its passing; they are too busy enjoying the feast of their own.

You and the rats eat each other, in a grisly circular feast, but you're outnumbered. Eventually, the rats win.

THE END

You continue your shamble through the pitch-black tunnel. Now, you don't have particularly good vision anymore anyway—there's a good possibility that there is currently some kind of worm occupying your left eye socket; at the very least, it gets really hard to see out of that eye sometimes, and there's a movement you're almost confident isn't from outside—but this tunnel is really dark. If you had an active sympathetic nervous system anymore, you'd probably be shivering from fear. But you don't, so you get a vague sense that maybe this pitch-dark place under the city isn't a particularly good place for a zombie to be.

You continue your walk, straight to the other side of the entrance. Luckily this side is a long steep slope rather than stairs, and you shuffle back up into the light.

You've popped out of the subway somewhere in the vicinity of Central Park. You meander into the grass, dragging your twisted foot behind and leaving a trail of crushed greenery. The remains of a jogger, identifiable only from the spandex shorts and foot-molded shoe attached to one bloody leg stump, line the walkway.

Ah, what a beautiful place.

You wander over to the edge of a pond. Model boats lie half-sunk in the shallows of the shining blue waters, abandoned by their owners in the beginning of the zombie plague panic. As a result, the waterway looks like it was struck by a fierce mini-tsunami, perhaps instigated by the giant ducks swimming contentedly in the pond.

Drawn by their movement and the possibility of a meal, you splash into the water after a duck with a bulbous red wattle, and are left in a bit of soggy zombie surprise when the waterfowl escapes you. It takes several attempts for you to get back out, and you wrench your back into an odd angle in your efforts to haul yourself ashore.

You try to take a bite out of the still man watching your pathetic duck hunt, only to break your teeth—apparently that human is neither alive nor a zombie, but made of metal. Your zombie grill now has an extra intimidation factor.

You hear an unusual sound—a sort of wooden rumbling and what might be a laugh. It draws your attention, and you ponderously shuffle over.

A horse, bloodied white carriage still dragging behind, is chewing the grass on the side of the paved path. It knickers and shies away as you approach.

You:

⊙ Eat those horsey brains. *Turn to page 210.*

(Choices continue on next page)

⊙ Just take a nibble. *Turn to page 211.*

⊙ Climb in the carriage. *Turn to page 213.*

⊙ Continue on. *Turn to page 214.*

The man wrenches the door open and tosses the girl inside. She screams and cries harder.

But he made a mistake. He turned his back to you and your kind.

You reach out, your cadaver-like hand latching on to the collar of his expensive white shirt, pulling him off his balance and away from the car. Your compadres reach, reach, reach, some of them also getting a handhold. He is resisting. You can hear his heart beating faster. You pull. He struggles.

The shirt rips, the collar coming clean off, and the man pulls away for a moment. You are too slow to react in time to stop him, but shuffle toward him again. The man has enough time to slam the door shut—the little girl inside screams louder, her face turning bright pink—and turn back to face you.

Some of your companions are pounding on the hood of the car, shaking it slightly. The man feels the tremors behind him and looks around nervously, but has decided the undead in front of him are a bigger threat. He is unarmed. You step forward again, moaning "uuugggghh." Your head lolls forward again, and you step closer. The man is looking back and forth, as if for an escape route, but all the zombies are closing in. You pull back your arm and swipe at him again, but you miss—he has climbed on top of the vehicle. You press closer to it, flailing your arms at him. The girl inside the car is screaming at the top of her lungs. The man is shouting—"ha! Huh!"—little barks in time with his kicks.

Kicking isn't nice. He shouldn't have done that.

When he kicks out at the undead executive businesswoman next to you, you grab his ankle before he can retreat. You have an iron grip, and all you have to do is pull down, down. He loses his balance and slams hard on top of the car. You must have stunned him a little, because he doesn't immediately get up again.

You pull him down, off the vehicle, and his patent leather shoe comes off in your hand. He kicks out at you and your zombie friends, but he's forgotten about the monsters on the other side of the car. Several hands grab his head and neck and shoulders and pull the other way.

But this is YOUR catch, and you pull, too.

The man begins to scream, zombies yanking on each of his limbs.

You feel it then, under your undead hands—his heartbeat, somewhere in his calf. He continues to struggle, but you don't mind. You pull the leg just a smidge closer and clamp your teeth down where the ankle begins to thicken. Your blunted front teeth draw blood.

The other monsters near you smell the blood or else feel the same thing you did, and they imitate you, biting until the man has mouth-sized tears everywhere he can be reached. After your first bite, you go back for a second, a little deeper this time.

The man screams, a sound that must be horrible to anyone still alive and listening—like his little girl, inside the car below. She begins to holler, too, a full-bodied yell of terror. She doesn't understand. You catch a glimpse of her, there on the seat not inches away, clutching her stuffed animal rear-end up. You snarl at her, and her eyes clamp shut and she screams again.

You continue pulling and biting on the leg you can reach.

It is a long while later that the man stops screaming.

Collectively, you and your kind pull the corpse down lower, sliding it down the hood of the vehicle. He lands on his stomach, eyes staring into the front seat.

A few of the others continue to eat, but the excitement of it is gone for you.

You:

⊙ Continue walking. *Turn to page 195.*

⊙ Chew on a neighbor. *Turn to page 196.*

There's something about those pigtails that attracts you, and you snatch at them with a clumsy hand. You miss—they are short, and move very quickly. Your swat draws the attention of the man though, and he drops the keys. He turns toward you, horror in his eyes.

The little girl screams, an ear-piercing sound that temporarily drives you and your monster kinsmen back for a half-shuffle.

She turns, and looks right at you—and somehow you see her. Not like you've been seeing her, as a tiny piece of still-breathing meat, but as a little girl.

It's very confusing, and you stop and stare. The girl stares back at you, sniffling. Her father is trying to ease himself down to the pavement to pick up the keys, so the girl on his hip sinks lower and lower in your sight.

You roll your head to one side.

Hm.

She IS really cute.

You aren't exactly functioning at optimum capacity right now, but somewhere in your sluggish brain, something… shifts.

You make a decision. Your body is slowly rotting and you can't so much as speak, but you make a decision: You are going to get that girl.

You moan and lurch forward. The father is crouched all the way down, and he has to make a decision, too—reach for the keys and let go of his daughter, or stand up without a method of escape and hold on to the child?

He lets go of the girl and grasps for the keys. She stands there, a nervous wail building in her chest. She is afraid, and so stands completely motionless, like a frightened rabbit. He is afraid, too, and he turns to look behind him, trying to see the keys.

That's when you move forward. You moan and grab the little girl around the waist with one arm. She screams that awful high shriek again, and her father shouts "NO!" and leans toward you. But it's too late; you already have her in your arms, and you aren't letting go.

You pull on the girl, and the father tries to pull her out of your hands. She thrashes, her little pigtails swishing in your face.

Maybe this would have worked out for the father, had it not been for the other zombies in the street. Now that he is out in the open, without the car to protect his back, he is truly surrounded. They reach for him.

He keeps trying to pull the girl from your arms, but now he has hands on his waist, pulling him, too. A zombie in a fast food hat bites down, hard, on the man's shoulder, and he reflexively reaches back with a cry, letting go of the girl.

You shuffle backward.

The man screams out "Lily!! Lily, my ba—"

The rest of his words are swallowed into an inhuman scream, as the fast food zombie bites the man's face. You and the girl see him fall into a crowd of the undead, his legs thrashing.

You moan softly. "Uugh."

The girl begins another hiccuping cry.

You don't know much—or anything, really—but some part of you decides that this adorable little creature is yours.

She wiggles in your arms and puts a hand around your neck, sucking her thumb, big wet tears staining both your cheeks.

You shift away whenever another of your kind comes closer, keeping the girl out of range, but for the most part, their attention is on the man being devoured. The girl is, almost literally, small potatoes.

You:

⊙ Go toward the building. *Turn to page 197.*

⊙ Turn down the alley. *Turn to page 199.*

⊙ Duck into a nearby storefront. *Turn to page 203.*

Look, zombies aren't exactly known for their intelligence, and you weren't exactly the best of the bunch in the first place. You mostly only respond to external stimuli.

Which is why, when faced with living prey you don't know how to grab, you start banging on the vehicle in front of you. You smash the trunk, ponderously, a monotonous thud-thud-thud drumbeat that shakes the car and slowly breaks the bones in your unfeeling hands.

The man has opened the door, and throws in the girl. You continue shuffling forward, hammering on the metal dully as you walk.

You watch through hazy eyes as the man throws a solid punch at a clean-shaven young zombie in front of him, and then at another as it moves in to bite him. He keeps backing up, and with a quick motion, sits in the car, practically on top of the girl—now red-faced from screaming—and pulls in his legs.

Several undead attackers lose fingers when he slams the door.

You continue moving along the car, rocking it as you rap on the roof—"Tap tap thud scraaaaaaape tap." Your hand is leaving bloody trails along the window as the man climbs over the middle steering gears and into the front seat. The little girl is sniffling into the stuffed unicorn, her knees drawn up to her chest.

You notice that the car shakes when you strike it, so this time you shove a little harder. The man looks up with alarm when he sees you shaking the sedan, then slams a key into the ignition and pushes on the gear.

The car jumps forward, throwing you back and over the roof at an angle, in a triple impact. Several other undead are also tossed about, and the car knocks over dozens more in the street like bowling pins.

You watch them leave from your view against the pavement. You can no longer get up; this body is too badly damaged. You begin to crawl, dragging your useless legs behind you, twisted to an odd angle.

You:

⊙ Chew on a neighbor. *Turn to page 196.*

⊙ Lie where you are. *Turn to page 202.*

There you go, just-a shamblin' down the street, moanin' uugh-ugh-guuuh—

Well, you never were much of a singer anyway. Tired of the scenery, you continue ambling down the road, not paying too much attention to the area. It's the journey, not the destination, that matters, right?

So you're ambling along, minding your own business, when you encounter a cluster of zombies in some sort of tussle. Before you even get to close, you see what's going on: A group of humans has organized, and they are fighting against the horde, armed with fire axes, pistols, a shotgun, and…what looks to be a shovel?

They are killing your kinsmen…permanently. The fight looks kinda intense.

You:

⊙ Keep walking, trying to avoid the fight. *Turn to page 207.*

⊙ Get in there and help your comrades! *Turn to page 208.*

With no more living prey in sight, you are stuck with the monotonous company of your undead peers. Sure, shuffling around, hanging out, moaning about un-life, is fine for a while, but then it just starts to seem so empty.

That's right. Being a zombie is boooor-ring.

Out of sheer spite, you approach the nearest former-human, a lightly decaying delivery truck driver in a brown outfit that can't have been flattering when he was alive and most certainly isn't now that he's dead. You follow him for a few idle minutes, sizing him up. Seems decent enough.

You take a bite.

Being a zombie himself, he feels only the pressure of your teeth, and perhaps notices that he is slightly diminished, but doesn't react overmuch. You chew as best as you can with a dislocated lower jaw. Hm. Gamey. A little sour.

Definitely not top-shelf stuff, but whatever. It's good to try new things, right?

You seem to be the only un-dead type to have figured out other zombs can be used for basic sustenance. Day by day, as the undead population is picked off or over-rotted, you manage to hold together, taking a nibble here and there whenever another monstrous creature comes close enough. It's easy lunch.

But your new diet isn't doing much for your figure. You don't have a proper digestive system anymore—at least not one that can efficiently break down decomposing flesh (mostly because it, too, is slowly rotting away). So the souring meat you've been eating is getting a bit backed up in your belly. After a few days, your gut is as big as a water buffalo's, and hangs nearly as low.

If you could feel, you might say you don't feel so good. But you don't, so you don't even particularly notice when the weather gets a bit warmer and your stomach swells with gases.

By mid-afternoon, you can't fit through doors. Your skin is distorted, stretching in globs like a melting candle.

All that gas has to go somewhere.

Eventually, you burst.

You dealt it, but you ain't gonna be around to smelt it.

THE END

The rest of the horde is too preoccupied with gnawing on rotting remains or practicing their moaning to notice as you lurch toward the nearest building. You shuffle-step, shuffle-step closer to the door. The girl twists in your arms, sniffling into your shirt and making you sway.

You stop. Stairs up to the door. Muscle coordination isn't really your thing recently.

You bend at the waist, mechanically, and the girl finds her feet on the concrete step and releases your neck. She's still super-cute, despite—or because of—her flushed pink cheeks and eyes shining with tears. Your cold heart palpates for a beat. She looks back into your eyes and reaches up to grip one of your mangled fingers in her chubby little hand, clinging tightly to the fluffy unicorn with the other.

Together, you climb the six stairs; you swaying each leg up, she stepping with the solid confidence of a toddler sure she has figured out this skill, stomping solidly on each step and making her princess-themed shoes light up—but still holding tight to your hand in case she slips. You moan your encouragement.

Several minutes later, you have achieved the summit. You roll your head to the right and look down at the girl. Together, you knock on the door, your heavy slaps the bass to the rat-tat-tat melody of her tiny fist.

There's movement in the blinds in the window next to the door. A moment later, the door opens the tiniest crack, and you can see the hint of green eyes.

"Auntie!" the girl says, and releases your hand to jump up excitedly.

The green eyes behind the door shift uncertainly, then the door opens slowly. The little girl tumbles inside and hugs the woman's leg with two arms.

The woman meets your glazed eyes and stares. There's a long pause, and she pushes the girl further inside the house. Then she says, simply, "Thank you."

You are almost feeling good about this. This moment has been the best of your un-life, you decide with the small part of your brain you have left. This was special.

It's because you are trying to contemplate your feelings that you don't notice the shotgun the woman has pulled from behind the door. You only happen to glance at it before she pulls the trigger and unloads a double-barrel of scattershot into your face from six inches away.

The force of the shot throws you off the stairs, and what's left of your cognition is blown out of your skull.

So much for trying to act against your nature.

M.E. KINKADE

THE END

You shuffle-step away from the berserk horde with a vague sense of a need to protect the child. The alley is dark and littered with small debris.

The girl is squirming in your arms, still sobbing lightly. Luckily for her, you died not too long ago, so the stench hasn't set in yet. Her movements make you sway with each step, slightly off-balance. You moan with irritation: "Eerrrggh."

She stops moving, freezing with fear.

That's better.

You drag your half-functioning body down the alleyway, unsuccessfully trying to dodge a black garbage bag. It gets caught on your twisted leg, and now you're dragging that, too. Great.

The kid starts to wiggle again, and maybe it would be better if you ate her. In fact, you're opening your maw to try when she starts up again with those big shining eyes, and you can't do it. You roll your head back and away, even though it keeps you from seeing the trash in front of you.

You put her down—best to keep temptation slightly removed—and creak back upright, muscles protesting. She looks up at you, as if startled by your behavior. You grunt and continue shuffling forward. You hear her small feet pattering after you a moment later.

As you reach the end of the alleyway, you grunt again, hoping the kid gets the clue. Either way, she stands back, and you stagger out, looking for other undead out of the corner of your half-lidded eyes.

You remember bits and pieces from your living days—not much, just snippets, really—but you know enough to know that the small one following you probably won't be eating human flesh. So you'll have to feed her something else.

With that concept held in your swiss-cheese brain, you reevaluate the street. Several houses down, the front door stands open. You'll have to cross the zombie horde and make it up the stairs, but that seems like a good enough location.

With staggered steps you turn back around to face your cute little problem. "Hiiii," she says, waving.

The cuteness actually bursts a couple of blood vessels in your brain (well, that could be the necropsy setting in, but you'll blame the cuteness). You moan "maaaaaaoogh" in response, and pick the child up again. Without the full range of motion in your arms, it's clumsy, and you tilt far forward, struggling to balance.

You stagger toward the house, dodging the nearby zombie, who, for their part, mostly continues dragging their feet and moaning. Not you. You've got responsibilities now.

Man, un-life's so hard for a parentally-inclined zombie.

It takes some serious work to get you and your bundled, squirming, adorable adoptee into the house. You'd be sweating if you were still capable. You plunk the kiddo in a cushioned chair a few shuffles near the door and moan at her to keep quiet—"maaaaauuuuugh." Hopefully she'll get the message.

You shuffle back, closing the door behind you. By flailing one of your claw-like hands at the door several times (and was that sound your finger breaking?), you manage to lock it.

There. Safe and sound.

You shuffle ponderously around the house, checking for any of the owners. From the blood smeared across the walls near the entryway and the entrails in the second bathroom, it's reasonable to assume they won't be returning. You close off that door, too (with considerably more effort—you definitely broke a few fingers), and wander back toward the front of the house.

While you were gone, the urchin made herself comfortable. She is sitting on the floor, scribbling on a book with a blue ink pen.

You leave her to it, and laboriously shuffle to the kitchen. When she hears you slamming open cabinet doors, she toddles in, her staggering run a miniature facsimile of yours. Aww.

Between the two of you, you pull out all the food from the shelves. When she discovers a box of Crunchy-Os and eats them messily (how did those get in her hair?!), you are satisfied that she isn't going to starve.

This whole child-rearing thing isn't easy when you are undead and beginning to decay, but it sure is inspiring. Yup. You and this kid—you call her "Ggrrghh" mostly—get along great. You spend your day shuffling around the house, playing with Ggrrghh and keeping her safe from the dangers outside. She eats cereal or candy, or a can of cooked beans that you smash open on the floor. After she finds the makeup left in the bathroom by the previous owner, she takes great care in painting your face with bright red lipstick, big circles of blush, and deep purple eyeshadow. She also likes a hat she found in the closet, and plunks it down on your head with all the finality of the next fashion superstar. You literally lack the heart to stop her. She does seem very pleased with the whole thing, but that flicker of cognition left in your brain tells you, when you pass a mirror, that you truly look like a monster now.

Some time after you woke from death (after the worms burst your stomach but before they had developed into full-grown flies), you and Ggrrghh are playing outside. There aren't many zombies around, and she hasn't been coping well with being kept inside all day.

And besides, she let herself out.

So you're outside when you see something that has become unusual—large vehicles driving down the street. You stare at them quizzically, rolling your heavy head from side to side on your weakening neck.

You:

⊙ Go inside. *Turn to page 204.*

⊙ Stay and watch. *Turn to page 206.*

Dragging your half-maimed carcass around is a lot of work. I mean, damn, what's a zombie gotta do to get a little help? The other nearby zombies continue wandering by, moaning. And what do they even have left to moan about? I mean, really, they're still ambulatory. #Firstworldzombieproblems, ya know?

You roll yourself onto your back and stare up into the sky. You know, this is actually kinda nice. The buildings on either side of you rise up to the heavens, seeming to hold up the sky. You can even see, in the distance, taller buildings, stretching even further up. Clouds amble by, and sometimes birds. It really is a beautiful day. Other zombies should take more time to appreciate this, rather than shambling along, moaning about their stupid problems.

You've got real proble—

Why is the ground shaking? What's that sound?

Next time, try to enjoy the view from somewhere other than the middle of a road. You've been run over by a van some numbskull has made into a zombie death trap. The barbed wire on the grill whiffed over your head, but that wasn't much of a relief when your ribcage caught on the undercarriage. Those bastards didn't even care. You are dragged along under the car for miles before they even bother to stop. Then they poke you—or what was left, which was little more than a meaty spinal cord and your head—with a stick to dislodge your remains.

And then, of course, they shoot you.

Damn it. Does no one have an appreciation for nature anymore?!

THE END

You grapple with your precious cargo all the way into the storefront nearby, which might have formerly been a laundromat—you aren't so good at building identification since the virus ate away most of your grey matter. Anyway, it's dark, secluded, and free from other un-life.

The perfect spot.

You look at the girl you're still holding with one arm (your elbow has locked into place again). Those chipmunk-round cheeks, bright shiny eyes, and perky little pigtails really are unbearably cute.

Unbearably. Cute.

Being a zombie, you don't bear it for long.

As if sensing that things are suddenly looking grim for her, the girl starts another wail, like a distant fire truck driving over shards of glass.

If there had been any hope left for her, that ended it.

You take a big bite out of her precious little apple cheek. With the other hand, you pull on a pigtail so hard it pulls off part of her scalp. Her eyes have gone wide with pain and blind terror, and she squirms to escape.

You take another bite, out of her teensy widdle shoulder this time.

Now that you've cornered this prey as all yours, you can take as long as you want. You particularly enjoy sucking the sweet baby-flesh off each wiggling finger and all 10 of her perfect toesies.

It's as true for monsters as for humans—baby-meat is for the particularly refined palate. You devour every last cutie-patootie bite.

Meal complete, you:

⊙ Continue your stroll down the street. *Turn to page 195.*

⊙ Follow it with an undead snack. *Turn to page 196.*

Remembering something fuzzy about the danger of small humans being near moving vehicles, you moan at Ggrrghh to come back inside. She bounds over to you, presenting you with a dandelion weed she found growing in the grass next to a decapitated police officer. How sweet!

You swipe a clumsy paw at it (not noticing you knocked the sappy weed to the ground), and shove Ggrrghh up the stairs as gently as you are able—she only scrapes her knee once this time (You're really getting the hang of this!).

When you're both inside, you lean against the door and Ggrrghh turns the lock, just as she learned. It takes her two hands, but the bolt slides satisfyingly into place. You nod and moan your approval, and Ggrrghh scampers away to draw on the walls or play in her own feces, whatever it is that kids do at this age.

By slapping at the shades, you part the blinds so you can look out, thumping your forehead against the window to get a good view. The vehicles are mottled green and brown and grey, and roll to a stop nearly right outside of your building. Figures in long white coats and heavy black vests clamber out, followed by people in clothes that match the trucks behind them. There aren't many zombies out right now, but the people herd them closer together with electric prods mounted on long sticks. By working in coordinated groups, the undead can't approach to bite anyone. A soldier jumps down out of the final vehicle and drags out a wide ramp. The cohort of zombies is herded up the ramp. One of the people in the white coats sometimes makes a motion to the soldiers, and one of the undead monsters is culled from the herd—and the ring of a shot echoes in the street.

You lean back from the window, wondering if you should hide, but the shot startled Ggrrghh and she begins to cry, toddling toward you with arms up for you to lift her (or let her climb you like a jungle gym, whatever the case may be). Outside, the people with the vans and trucks look startled, and a group breaks off to approach your house.

You try to moan to Ggrrghh to make her stop, but she won't be consoled. She shakes her head and sniffles big crocodile tears.

"Hey, anybody in there?" a male voice asks harshly.

Ggrrghh gasps and toddles toward the door. She may be short, but dangit if those little legs aren't fast. You can't catch her before she is at the door, gripping the lock with her two chubby hands. She opens the door.

You can't get a good view, what with your decaying vitreous humor and the poor angle, but the soldier at the door looks shocked to see Ggrrghh.

She babbles at him in incomprehensible happy toddler talk, and then comes running toward you. She's tugging on your dislocated thumb excitedly, pointing at the door, when the soldier sees you.

This time, shock is most definitely an understatement. He raises his weapon and aims it at you, but lowers it as Ggrrghh continues babbling at you. You roll your head to the left and moan at her sweetly.

The soldier and his two support units stare in unmitigated bafflement.

One says, "Little girl, come here, we'll protect you now," and crouches and opens her arms to greet Ggrrghh. When the toddler sees this, however, she hides behind your leg, only barely peeking out.

"Get Dr. Higgins," the man with the gun whispers to the soldier who had tried to collect Ggrrghh. There are a few tense moments, then an older man, grey flecking his black curls, steps into the room and assesses the situation.

"You're telling me this specimen is guarding a human child?" Dr. Higgins' voice is cool, clinical. "How interesting."

Dr. Higgins steps closer and stares you in the eyes. "Thank you for looking after this girl. She needs to be with her own kind now. Please give her to us."

You shift your balance, not trusting these new people. Then you reach back and gently propel Ggrrghh toward the waiting soldiers.

Dr. Higgins watches with great interest. "Fascinating," he says. "Is she yours?"

"Uughh," you say. It's close enough to the truth, anyway.

The researcher nods, considering. "Will you come with us, please? You see, we are developing a cure for the plague, and as you seem to have a certain resistance to it…"

Though Dr. Higgins is being extremely polite (something there's been a distinct lack of since the horde rose up), you realize this isn't a proper question. You're going with him whether you like it or not.

You moan agreement.

Dr. Higgins and his team load you into the trucks with the other undead. It turns out he's set up a lab in a wing of the city morgue. You cooperate with his tests, and in time, he develops a cure. He even administers it to you in his gratitude.

You regain some mental cognition, but there's not much he can do for the damage already done to your body, so you are again intelligent enough to truly appreciate agony. There aren't enough painkillers in all the world to deal with this kind of damage. Dr. Higgins puts you out of your misery.

A year later, you and Dr. Higgins share the Nobel Prize in Biochemistry. Yay for you—this time, you're really dead.

THE END

Foresight has never really been your thing—even before this whole "not-alive" thing kicked in. So as the armored trucks start rumbling down the street, you don't get up or wonder what is going on—you're a freakin' zombie, you stand there making moany noises.

Little Ggrrghh seems to be having a grand ole' time playing in the garbage in the street, but she is observant, so she does notice the cars.

"Twucks!" she cries out, giddy as a filly in her first rodeo. She bounces up and down, so excited she can't contain herself. "Wook!" she says, "wook, twucks!!!" She gestures frantically for you to look at the trucks, so you roll your head in that direction and grunt. "Ugugh…"

That seems to satisfy her, but she's still too energized. She runs down the street to greet the incoming vehicles, hollering "twucks, twucks!" all the way.

You moan again. Kids. All they seem to do is go running off somewhere, always making you chase them.

That's how you end up moaning, arms extended in front of you in classic movie-monster style, chasing the toddler down the street. Her yelling is so enthusiastic as to be easily confused with terrified.

Upon reflection, it's not really that surprising why the National Guardsman shot you. You're not mad, just disappointed, because sweet little Ggrrghh, with whom you thought you had such a nice bond, doesn't even notice as you die for the second time.

Kids. They never appreciate the sacrifices you make for them, do they?

THE END

Look, fighting isn't really your scene, particularly when there's an indication that you might lose.

You moan quietly to yourself and skirt the edges of the crowd, at one point flattening yourself against a brick building (as best you can, anyway) to avoid the swings of what might have formerly been a baseball bat but is now mostly a club full of splinters. Then you get clipped by a partially dismembered zombie. The nasty thing even tries to take a bite out of you, how rude!

You've nearly made it out of the crowd and to the relative quiet beyond. You try to shuffle quietly so no one notices you. Don't mind me, just a zombie goin' for a walk!

And you would have gotten away with it, too, if it weren't for those meddling kids—right before you make it to safety, a group of thugs with their saggy jeans and hippity-hop music rounds the corner armed with chains, more guns, and a comically large stereo.

They're indiscriminate with their violence, and even though you were merely a regular monster minding your own business, you're decapitated by a 16-year-old with a grudge.

THE END

It's one thing when it's a totally fair fight between two groups—and your undead compatriots are winning, of course—and an unfair and unjustified attack where it looks like you might lose. I mean, don't they know that the zombies always win? Fighting back with weapons is, like, discrimination or something.

So you wade—er, drag yourself—into the fray. The human fighters are in a tight group, weapons pointed outward in a semi-circle as the zombie horde encroaches and tries to go in for a bite. When a particularly bold or clumsy one does, it is bludgeoned, shot, or chopped until it falls or gets back out of the way. Two undead are amputated at the neck while you watch, their heads rolling away and getting stuck in the storm drain.

All right. Time for a really awesome zombie to join the fight. You try to crack your knuckles in anticipation, but only manage to dislocate your right index finger. It sticks out at an odd angle as you step up to the fighting crowd.

You stand in the middle of the crowd of zombies and begin moaning orders.

"Ugh! Arrughh, moggh errhh oooonnng," you say. All the humans and some of the zombies look at you in utter confusion. Public speaking never has been your strong suit.

"Oorrghh!" you moan, leaning hard left as you do. A handful of the undead crowd understands, and the fighting on the left-hand side of the circle is a bit more intense than the right-hand side.

"Orrk aahh. Rrrrgghh!" you moan, leaning right. Four of the zombies on that half jump in as the left-hand zombies fall back.

After a few more moans in this way, you get some momentum; the zombies surge and fall, like flesh-eating waves, breaking up the organization of the human fighters.

"Gguugh!" you say, proud of your fighters. Maybe you can be the leader of a zombie gang or something. That might be cool. "Oiughh, ahherg!"

The zombies on the left have managed to drag out one of the human fighters, throwing the middle-aged man into the fervent crowd. The zombie attackers that stop to consume him—to the horror of his human friends—are quickly replaced by other, fresher undead.

With your newfound zombie coordination (who knew such a thing was possible?!), your group of horror-movie monsters turns the tide. One human, apparently out of ammo, throws the pistol uselessly at you in her zombie-induced fear. Excellent. Your fighters have no such emotional problems—or emotions at all.

Things are going really well, and it looks like all the remaining undead are going to wander off with full stomachs, when the cavalry arrives.

Literally. Who knew there were this many mounted police officers in New York?

They come down the street, horses nearly flank to flank, the cops in crisp blue uniforms each carrying a pistol. Unfortunately, they have good aim, too. All around you, the heads of the zombies explode like water balloons. Just before you can dive into the relative safety of a 14-year-old wielding a baseball bat, a passing bullet clips you in the shoulder and you go down.

You feebly crawl toward the fleshy humans, but the distraction was all they needed, and the pre-teen makes your head into target practice.

THE END

If a 150-pound human makes a good meal, a 1,100-pound horse has got to be some kind of ultimate zombie feast. You can practically feel its massive heartbeat in your shriveling blood vessels.

"Mmmoaoohhggh," you moan excitedly.

The horse, an animal so white it could be a stand-in for a unicorn, stares at you with wide eyes and tries to shy away, jostling the carriage it pulls. You drag yourself closer, and the horse whinnies and backs up a few steps, skidding slightly on the walkway.

You don't have much experience with this sort of thing, eating horses. Up close, it looks even bigger. Where does a zombie begin?

You stagger toward it head-on. If you had any brainpower left, you might imagine that juicy big grey matter behind that long nose. As it is, you mostly continue on a crash course toward wherever you're moving.

The horse backs up again, nostrils flaring, and neighs loudly. Gimmie a break, it's not like the undead get a chance to shower much. Jerk horse.

You moan and lurch toward the horse.

Something you didn't consider—because, again, zombie—was that a 1,100-plus pound animal might be able to stop you. So you're rather taken aback when the horse rears on its hind legs, lashing out at you with its heavy, metal-reinforced front hooves.

A healthy human's head can be pummeled like a soccer ball by a horse. A necrotic, rotting zombie's head, apparently, gets squished like an overripe grape.

Heigh-ho, Silver, you're stomped dead.

THE END

You're not overly hungry, and back when you were human your mom always taught you not to waste your food, so you only want a bit of horse. You know, so you can tell your undead friends (as soon as you make them) that you've had it once. It's probably a delicacy.

The horse is big, taller than you, so you stagger over at an angle. The white horse tosses its mane and sidesteps, but it's constrained by the carriage. You lean down, back popping, and take a bite out of its meaty back thigh.

The horse doesn't like that, and screams its annoyance, but you are safe on the side as it kicks and thrashes. You stagger slightly away, satisfied with your taste. The horse kicks, and with a horribly loud CRACK one side of the carriage breaks loose, leaving the carriage only half-attached to the harness.

Over the next several hours, the horse grows weaker. The other half of the carriage breaks when the white steed collapses, further injuring the animal with a long cut to its flank. The horse dies, as is the way of these things—but a few hours after that, it gets back up again, shaking its mane in its new un-dead incarnation.

"Neighhghghg," it says.

Congratulations. You've got a zombie horse.

You've stayed nearby this whole time, exploring the nooks and crannies of the park, and the horse's moan draws your attention back.

It takes some doing and at least a few dislocated bones, but you mount your fierce undead beast.

You were hoping it would look triumphant, like a conquering general lording his victory over his newly subjugated peoples, but in reality you are mostly staying on by benefit of the horse's sagging backbone. You lay nearly prone on its back, pulling on the reins with one clenched hand. The horse itself takes on a slightly greenish-black tinge as necropsy sets in. Truly a warrior's ride.

So transported, you ride throughout the city. Your zombie horse is awesome. The huge beast can take a lot more damage than a human zombie, and more than a few encounters with living humans result in a minor bullet wound for the beast and a crushed body for the attacker.

This horse is probably an ancestor of some really badass horse, like Bucephalus or Black Beauty. And that's probably why when, weeks later when the zombies clearly outweigh the number of surviving humans, you are named—well, moaned—the leader of the zombie uprising. I mean, no other zombie had the courage, intellect, or general mobility to ride a zombie horse, so you are clearly a superior specimen.

Your reign is a long and fruitful one. You and your trusty steed oversee the largest zombie epidemic ever known. On your permanent death bed, when your limbs are so rotted you are reduced to a pile of bones barely held together with ligaments and rotted muscle, you moan "stroungghas." After your second death, the humans begin to retake the zombie-held lands. Never again is there such a great undead empire.

THE END

The carriage has three steps to the ground, but it takes a bit of wrangling for you to get inside while the horse is fidgeting and tossing its mane. As you lean in, the horse backs up and bumps the carriage down and off the pavement. You collapse into the carriage with a WHUMP, and the horse, startled by the sound or the smell of your rotting carcass or who-knows-what, leaps forward. You spend the first minute or two of your carriage ride being thrown about the bottom of the carriage, still slippery with the blood of its former owner. The horse runs at a full gallop, and you're jostled enough to twist your wrist in a disturbing way, but eventually you clamber into the seat.

The horse, still spooked by your presence, runs until its sides heave, and eventually slows to a canter. You stare out of your foggy eyes at the foliage around the park, and the breeze of your passage makes your ears flap. (Only because you sink lower in the chair does your left ear remain intact).

What a lovely day.

Eventually your terrified equine wears itself out, but not before you're well out of Central Park. The second turn the horse makes on the streets is crowded with zombies, and the animal panics and backs away. The bump over the curb jostles you out of the carriage, and you land gracefully on your face.

You:

⊙ Eat that jerk. *Turn 210.*

⊙ Bite the horse so you can maintain your speedy transit. *Turn to page 211.*

⊙ Shamble up and continue your journey. *Turn to page 214.*

You walk along, stumbling into metal garbage cans and weaving through the stopped traffic clogging some of the roads. You moan a greeting to other zombies as you pass, and they share your blank-eyed stare. Every so often, the sound of a human screaming their last breath rings out, sometimes accompanied by a scattering of gunshots.

You've wandered a long way, but you're forced to stop by a metal guardrail. If anyone nearby could operate a camera, you would have your picture taken with the tiny Statue of Liberty behind you, a classic photo-op. As it is, you won't even remember having been here. You shuffle through Battery Park, nearly tripping over an abandoned blanket littered with knockoff handbags. One catches on your ankle and makes a fetching fashion accessory for your lower half. Without knowing it (of course), you've wandered to the lowest point of Manhattan Island.

You:

⊙ Shamble into the Hudson River. *Turn to page 216.*

⊙ Cross the Brooklyn Bridge. *Turn to page 217.*

⊙ Turn back into the city. *Turn to page 218.*

The animal lets out another chest-rattling roar, and then another answers. Two! Two giant beast-things!

This fence isn't so bad, really. You lean forward, reaching for the lions and moaning back at them as they roar. But you've overextended, and you tip into the exhibit.

That would be troubling if you felt pain or were alive—the sharp points of the fence left holes in your abdomen—but you're a mindless monster motivated by a desire to bite things, so you don't mind. You don't even mind that you just fell end-over-end down a concrete gully, breaking several bones.

Nope. As a zombie, all you care about is that it is now considerably harder to shuffle toward your destination. Your limbs are no longer moving in a coordinated fashion, and you flail like a duck in Jell-O.

Turns out it's been a coupla days since the zookeeper fed the lions—apparently a zombie uprising will cause all kinds of complications like that—and King and Queen Jungle are quite peckish.

Mmm, rotting meat, their favorite. Still moving, too! Oh joy!

The male lion is braver (or hungrier) and cautiously climbs down the embankment. You flail an arm, and the lion sniffs it unhurriedly. Not wanting to miss the fun, the female slides down, too. Her jaws fit perfectly around your misshapen head.

The male steps forward, gingerly taking your throat in his jaws, but, being a zoo lion, he's not used to his food moving at all, much less trying to eat him. The bite you take out of his jowl enrages him, and he releases your throat to step back and slam a massive paw at your head. Good thing you're already more or less brain dead, eh?

Still, he's dislocated your jaw. You continue to try to work it, but it's no good.

The lions settle in to enjoy their meal. So nice of you to drop in.

THE END

You've never been one for barriers or obstacles. You shamble onto one of the tourism boats near the park, and then right over the side.

Luckily, you don't need to breathe and don't feel the cold, so you don't mind being underwater. It's sort of liberating. The water near the city is murky, but—when you touch the bottom—you continue shuffling on. You pass bags of litter, old tires, pieces of old ships from the 17th century, and at least two corpses, their legs knee-deep in cement blocks. You wave to your boney kinsmen, causing you to lift off the river bottom and float a ways. You soon find that you can propel yourself along with the current this way, and you glide on out toward the sea.

Further out, the visibility improves, and you see some aquatic life. For the most part, they—being accustomed to strange creatures of all types and specialties—take no notice of you. Sometimes a passing eel takes a bite of you; sometimes you return the favor.

You continue on, slowly exploring the sea floor as you shamble along near the bottom, weighed down by the accumulated detritus that has snagged on your legs or feet. By the time you reach the icier depths, your path has gone dark. Aside from the occasional biting fish, however, the cold temperatures keep necropsy away, extending your un-life by many years.

That is how you became the first former-human to explore the Mariana Trench. Too bad all you can share with the rest of us is enlightened information like, "Ughhashuugh."

THE END

You continue walking, shuffling along toward the iconic Brooklyn Bridge. By now you look a sordid mess. It's more than the rotting flesh and various wounds on your person; your clothes are torn and an overall brown-black color from the filth you've been wading through, and various debris drags along behind you with every step—a knockoff purse, a plastic trash bag, a string of broken Christmas lights.

In other words, you're truly horrific.

The humans have gotten organized during your stroll. Near the opening of the bridge, cars form a long and tight barrier, without even enough room between them for a person—or zombie, whichever—to pass through them. You climb over, limbs flailing for purchase. Several times you go sliding off the edge, landing with a crash on the car adjacent.

Eventually you surpass the vehicular blockade, and are free to shuffle along the length of the bridge. You aren't alone, but a few zombies have already made this journey before you. Despite massive damage to their corpses, they continue to crawl. One disfigured monster, having been shot somewhere in the face, walks blindly over the edge of the bridge. He makes no sound as he falls, and the splash of his impact seems far distant.

At the end of the bridge are military personnel, bristling with expensive weaponry.

A shot rings out, echoing off the tall buildings—you are hit in the shoulder and stagger back with the impact but continue walking forward. The humans at the end of the bridge shout to one another, then suddenly you are at the end of a firing line, the target for 36 separate bullets. They rip into your flesh, causing your body to lurch and jump like you're electrocuted. Your right leg falls off completely, and you fall flat on the concrete. But you've still got arms, so you keep crawling.

It takes 79 shots, in total, before you are stopped, not five feet from the other side of the bridge. After watching footage of this encounter with you taken via helicopter, the head of FEMA decides to blow up bridge access to Manhattan Island. The city is abandoned to the zombies. It is assumed there are no human survivors—the poor souls that are still alive don't last more than a handful of days.

THE END

You turn to go back where you came from. Maybe now you can see the rest of Manhattan. Despite having been here for years when you were alive, you rarely saw much of the city as a whole, and, if you're honest with yourself, you saw most of that via the subway or staring outside of a cab. For the first time, you are seeing the sights. Granted, you're already dead, so you won't be crossing anything off your bucket list, but still.

You have the esteemed privilege of being a zombie that didn't do much of anything. You aren't particularly interested in eating people or animals; you don't go exploring too much; you just are.

You continue mindlessly wandering the island of Manhattan in true zombie monster form, and so are vaporized with the rest of New York when Russia, deciding the zombie plague is too much of a threat to deal with in typical ways, breaks all treaties with the United States and nukes the place.

It's a bit like bringing an Uzi to a knife fight. The Russian solution undeniably works, though the entire Eastern Seaboard has to deal with the repercussions for a century more.

The Russian who pushed the button is given the Nobel Peace Prize the next year.

THE END

You were always the lazy sort, even in life, so it's not particularly surprising that you'd go for the easier meal in un-life.

The aviary is a few steps away, and you moan happily as you walk. You crash through the decorative underbrush for a while, seriously confusing the vultures who see movement but smell death, until you careen into the swinging double-door entrances.

You are in a magical wonderland of birds, birds of every sound and color, magnificent in their beauty—but you are substantively unappreciative. No, you just fumble around, trying to catch one with loose-limbed swipes.

Unsurprisingly, the birds are both faster and smarter than you. Eventually, you wander back out of the aviary, having acquired nothing but heaps of sticky white bird shit in your hair and on your rotting person. Yummy.

You shuffle on, destroying several carefully plotted plant beds in Central Park. You come crashing out of the underbrush, emerging on a clear expanse of asphalt. It takes several more steps before you step clear of the brambles and sticks, and you moan happily.

Up ahead, movement.

It's a blond man, wearing a torn suit and leather loafers, sitting in a tree along the side of the road. You think to yourself, "aslkjerhff." You head toward him. He's sobbing and clinging to the small trunk.

"I knew I shouldn't have lived in New York," he cries. "All the monster movies are set in New York. I shouldda known better! Why? Oh why?!"

The part of your hole-riddled brain that used to enjoy watching television (thus creating some of the very holes making you who you are today) is trying to tell the rest of your brain that this pathetic noisy meat is none other than TV phenom and former-child-star Nelson Faris, but the message doesn't go far, and all the neurons on the other side of your mind get is "N--lll Hsss," which your language center interprets as "BRAIIIIIINS."

And that, boys and girls, is how zombie neuroscience works.

You're under Nelson's tree, and he's lucky you're lacking in motor control, because you're having trouble reaching him even though his foot is dangling just overhead.

"Oh please oh please," he says to you. "I have the two most adorable kids in the world! I've got to live! Think of the children!"

Which, of course, you don't.

"Please God I'll do anything," the film and TV star beseeches the heavens. "Let me survive this and I'll do anything. I'll sacrifice my acting career! What do you want from me!?"

You want:

⊙ BRAAAAAAINS. *Turn to page 221.*

⊙ Oooh shiny object! *Turn to page 222.*

Television and an infectious disease rotted your mind, so it's no surprise you don't recognize a film star. You only see lunch.

Nelson continues howling and crying to heaven, the police, anybody, but you're relentless. You keep swiping at his feet: you have to give up when your ligaments disconnect, whereas Nelson will eventually get tired of clinging to that branch. You latch onto a swinging foot and get a swift kick to the face in return. A few teeth are knocked loose and your nose breaks, but that isn't going to stop you. You're a mad dog with a treed cat, and you're not going anywhere.

Nelson sings to himself for a while, fighting off sleep. If music soothed the savage zombie, his singing would probably do the trick, but you've always been more interested in pop music than show tunes.

The sun sets and rises again, but you finally get your quarry. Nelson's hands go limp with exhaustion, and a foot—now shoeless, you've been gnawing on the leather for the past 5 hours or so—slips down out of the tree. The slobbery black leather falls from your slavering jaws, and you grab Nelson's hanging limb.

He struggles, weakly, but it's all over. You drag the multiple Golden Globe nominee and two-time Oscar host out of the tree and devour him, suit and all.

Your feasting attracts other undead, and you fight over his corpse. Your belly becomes distended with his innards.

You belch hugely. If any passerby were still functioning, they might have noted your burp was on-key, but as it is, your celebrity encounter just gives you mild indigestion.

Now, being quite well-fed, you:

◉ Continue the direction you were headed previously. *Turn to page 195.*

◉ Spend some quality time with your zombie mates. *Turn to page 224.*

You are distracted by a shiny object across the street, and shamble away to investigate. While you're gnawing on the tin can that had been tumble-weeding down the street, Nelson Faris climbs out of the tree and runs to the nearest building. The door opens before he can knock, and a tall handsome man hugs Nelson fiercely.

You're realizing something has happened behind you and are coming back across the street when Nelson stops, stares at you, and says, "I won't forget this."

You spend the next few weeks wandering the streets of New York, eating other zombies, or vermin, or humans when you can. You're shambling along, minding your own mindless business, when a limo with dark tinted windows pulls up alongside.

A window rolls down. "There, that's the one!" Nelson says, leaning out and pointing at you. You shamble toward him, perhaps to chew on his extended finger, when two burly men grab you from under each arm and shove you in the trunk. It's fairly roomy in there, and you spend most of the ride chewing on the tire iron (and some of it biting the flesh off your forearm).

When the car stops, the trunk opens, and the burly men funnel you into a chain-link cage. You lean into the metal, chewing lazily.

"This is the one," Nelson says. "I just think we could have a real hit on our hands! Just look! We can call it 'Dead and Loving It.' It'll be a sitcom, with me and my zombie pal trying to get along in tough New York City!"

"So you're saying it would basically be 'Will & Grace' meets 'Monster Movie,' eh?" a shorter man answers, considering.

"And you wouldn't have to pay the zombie anything!" Nelson says. He's really into this idea. "Just a few simple precautions to keep it from eating anyone, and it wouldn't be a big deal at all!"

"I love it," the plump man says, shaking Nelson's hand.

You and Nelson star in the next TV phenomena. It's a hit with housewives and the undead, and the ratings are pure Nielsen gold, considering there's only one big media company left still broadcasting. It turns out most of the audience can't even tell you're dead, and you are flooded with marriage proposals, are followed by the paparazzi (and no one minds if you bite them), and are even asked to host the Emmys.

But every acting career has its fall after a rise. Yours comes with extensive decomposition. By the end of season four, you are teeming with wriggling fly larvae, flesh-eating beetles, and cockroaches. Several of your makeup artists have quit, saying they never wanted to work in the industry if it meant applying false flesh to a monster that tries to bite their fingers and is totally unappreciative. More and more of your scenes are filmed with a stand-in. The audience doesn't even seem to notice.

You are put out to ignominious pasture, where the final stages of decay take over. Your bones are left lying in the open field behind the set.

THE END

Y ou're pretty popular in zombie circles after sharing your meal with them.

"Ughhh," says one, as you pass, and the other zombies all turn and look at you in what might be respect. You shrug it off. No big deal.

You start hanging with a regular zombie crew of sorts. You move in a loose pack, hunting, if not together, at least in general proximity. A zombologist might note that this pack behavior increases your kill rate, but then she'd probably also be running for her life from the cannibalistic monsters, so maybe not.

You're like sharks, moving in tandem together, restless predators who stop for nothing.

This phenomenon is being replicated on the other side of the tracks, too. Those zombies tend to be the fastest of the group, and their gang zips along the streets, a thunderous pack dealing death to whomever they find.

It is perhaps inevitable that one day your two groups meet. Your monsters stare down the opposing zombies. The bones of the assembled undead snap and crunch with a rhythmic musicality. The tension is rising.

You:

⊙ Keep walking. There's more than enough New York to go around. *Turn to page 225.*

⊙ Lead your brothers in a fight to defend your territory! *Turn to page 226.*

You've never been much for musicals, so you continue on your way, leaving your undead comrades to sort things out for themselves.

You meander down a few dark alleyways and up some stairs. Zombies don't read well (or at all) and you walk straight into a manhole. Good thing you can't feel those broken legs!

You continue shuffling along in sludge up to your waist (or is your waist down in the sludge? Hard to tell anymore). Up ahead is a branch in the tunnel.

You:

    ⊙ Take the left branch. *Turn to page 227.*

    ⊙ Take the right branch. *Turn to page 228.*

    ⊙ Stay where you are. *Turn to page 229.*

You've grown accustomed to being able to hunt in your neighborhood wherever you like, and you aren't particularly interested in allowing these upstart challengers onto your territory. You moan at the others, and a chorus of moans fills the air.

You won't be backing down.

The leader of the other group, a formerly tough-looking young guy in a leather jacket, moans as well.

Looks like it's time for a zombie rumble.

The two groups begin an elaborate dance (the Shuffle), neither side wanting to give ground. Zombies take to mindless violence like cats to napping, so it was probably a matter of time before you turned on one another.

The ensuing fight involved a lot of biting, sour flesh ripping from bones. It also happened in near-slow-motion, and was highly uncoordinated. The attackers were as likely to bite off the ear of someone from their gang than the opposing side.

The humans who pulled up in their armored tank must not have known what to think of the scene, because soldiers stopped and watched for a while, guns unslung but loose in their arms. They almost didn't need to fire on the zombie horde; you were doing such a good job ripping into your undead kin.

But then a few monsters, drawn to the heartbeats of the excited soldiers, peeled off from the fight and began dragging themselves, jaws snapping, toward the humans, and someone got nervous. No one was ever sure who fired that first shot, but in a blink the scene transformed into a field of zombies being mowed down by automatic weapons, annihilated before a strong, more determined, less decomposing foe.

THE END

You go sloshing off into the dark, nibbling on rats sometimes, but generally minding your own undead business.

After awhile, you realize you aren't alone in the dark anymore. You feel the heartbeats of someone—no, someones—before you see their small light. There are two of them, wearing smelly coveralls, and they are moving slowly. Perfect targets. You haven't had a decent meal down here in weeks!

You shamble toward them, giddily, and, being undead, you don't notice that they aren't showing a particular fear response. In fact, they aren't running and screaming at all. They're standing and waiting.

You rush them, splashing murky water with each shuffled step. At the last minute, one throws a net over you, hampering your feet. You come crashing to the ground, filth filling your nose and mouth, suffocating you. You thrash wildly.

Your attackers haul you up and out of the sewer. Up in the city, most of the zombie threat has been pacified. In fact, most were wiped out. It turns out that those undead that remain—that's you—have become sought-after pets for the wealthy, with a particularly brisk online black market.

Your attackers have turned a decent profit already, but the pickings are getting slim. They heard your sloshing around in the sewer and were down there, hunting you. And you ran right into their trap.

They strap you to a table and pull out your teeth with pliers. You'd be personally offended, if you were aware of such things, but they give you chicken bones with some meat still on, and then you stop attacking them quite so aggressively. They hose you down and dress you in plastic bandages they got from the Halloween store so you look more authentic. Then they pop you in a box and ship you overnight to China.

You are the crowning figure in the Communist Party's Presidential menagerie, moaning and drooling on yourself until a protest group breaks you out, claiming you represent the people of China under the Communist Party. The government responds with restraint, dropping bombs on only three area villages where it is believed you may be held, and the protest goes viral on YouTube.

THE END

The right-hand passage has a slight elevation, and before long you've emerged out of the smelly dark and are back on the streets of Manhattan.

As has been noted, zombies aren't particularly good at obeying road signs, so it's not too much of a surprise when you fail to stop before entering the construction zone. Perhaps because you've been slogging through sewage, you don't even notice when the pavement underneath you begins to seep into your shoes. You keep plowing through, leaving drag marks in the fresh cement, until your slow pace is brought to a standstill.

You've made yourself a new pair of concrete shoes, and your weak muscles are no longer strong enough to lift your feet. You try, but your ankle dislocates. You're not going anywhere.

The cement hardens, leaving you a permanent fixture in the city.

Later, when the work crews have cleared out most of the other zombies, the decision is made to leave you where you are, as a reminder to the population of the dangers of chemical warfare. A metal fence is added around your corpse, keeping passerby out of arms' reach, and you remain as an unliving monument in the City for years to come.

THE END

You're not much for making decisions one way or another, so you stop where you are, sloshing around in raw sewage with the rats. Sometimes you eat one, but there's plenty of refuse for a zombie to gnaw on if one's not too picky. And you're definitely not.

Down here, no one runs from you. No one fears you. You don't even have to compete with other zombies for resources. Nope, it's just you, the rats, a million gallons of waste, and the dark. It's downright peaceful.

Over time, the humans figure out how to eradicate the zombie threat. Life upstairs returns to normal, day by day. Soon there's hardly a trace left of the zombie uprising. It's calm, and people feel safe again.

Parents tell their children to say away from the storm drains "because a zombie might get you," believing the threat has long passed. But every so often, someone goes missing, and children sometimes claim they see something moving in the dark.

THE END

(OR IS IT?!!!!)

(It is.)

ABOUT THE AUTHOR

M.E. Kinkade wanted to be an architect when she was in third grade, but that didn't work out, so now she builds (and destroys) imaginary worlds instead. She lives in Dallas, Texas, and would absolutely be toast in the event of a real zombie outbreak. This is her first book.

Find her on Twitter @MEKinkade or at her website, mekinkade.com.

Printed in Great Britain
by Amazon